BARK!

By
Darrell Bain

Including the Autobiography of 'Tonto' the real-life addled little
daschund who inspired the story.

📖

Published by LL-Publications www.ll-publications.com © 2008
Cover image by Helen E. H. Madden www.pixelarcana.com © 2008

This book is dedicated to the memory of Gordon Rutt, a true friend and a really unique character. I miss him a lot. And to Biscuit and Tonto, two totally different but distinctly unique doggie people.

D.B.

Contents

BARK!

1

The meteorologists were all so completely fooled it was embarrassing. They didn't just make a wrong forecast; that happened with regularity anyway. This time they raised their erroneous weather forecasting to new heights of inaccuracy. It was on a day in late fall, with no fronts anywhere near, with the waters in the Gulf of Mexico no longer hot enough for hurricane formation, with no signs of a tropical storm apparent, with no weather patterns coming in from Mexico or the Pacific and with the whole state of Texas enjoying warm, balmy and cloudless weather. Suddenly a vicious low-pressure system formed over East Texas with the rapidity of a striking rattler. In an area about a hundred miles north of Houston, and fifty to a hundred miles wide, near hurricane-force winds suddenly sprang up and began ripping through the countryside in a counter-clockwise movement.

Trees blew over, power lines went down, commuters were caught on their lunch hour or while shopping with no protection and no warning. Fortunately, there were few casualties; Texans are used to sudden changes in the weather, but even the old-timers had to admit this one was a little too abrupt for their tastes, Texas weather or not.

For a solid hour the gusty winds blew in the counter-clockwise motion around the center of the low pressure as if a tropical storm had sprung up from nowhere. The meteorologists went mad trying to explain how this could be happening when there was so little moisture available to work with, a required ingredient for that type weather system. In fact, it never rained a drop the whole time. And then, just as suddenly as the weather had changed, it went back to normal, leaving debris strewn on yards, roads and highways, and a number of motor vehicle accidents caused by high winds and junk on the highways as the only sign it had ever existed.

Some meteorologists claimed to their dying day that it *hadn't* existed. It was impossible; therefore it hadn't happened. Others conveniently forgot about it, putting it out of their minds and going on about their business, as if by not thinking about the phenomena it could be relegated to the same category as forgotten names, dates or the times in high school they had embarrassed themselves by being turned down for a date or tripping over their own feet on the dance floor at the prom. Others remembered and made conscientious efforts to find an explanation for the oddity. They studied past weather patterns, fiddled with the exotic equations peculiar to their science, and ran all the data again and again through their super-duper fast weather computers, but for all their sweat and mental effort, wound up none the wiser afterwards.

In contrast, a few meteorologists in the Pentagon knew more than their fellows. They were the rare breed who studied upper atmospheric phenomena, the patterns and shifts of the jet stream and even farther up, the mechanisms which made weather work on the fringes of space; if that thin mix of charged particles, the streams of sun-stuff that managed to elude the Van Allen belts, could be called weather. Those men and women needed every bit of data they could garner in order to program the missiles and spy satellites and space launches and experiments the military was constantly conducting. They knew right off that something was badly awry.

Just as the out-of-nowhere low-pressure system was forming, several of the radars that monitored the near space environment picked up an anomaly. It was somewhat akin to the play of upper atmospheric lightning and trails of charged particles left in the wake of satellite launches, but different. In the mist of the sudden whorl of thin clouds not even visible to the naked eye, one meteorologist thought he detected something solid, or so it appeared; yet within the blink of an eye it was gone. If there hadn't been a recording of the phenomena, and if the military computers hadn't been programmed to flag anomalies, it would have been missed entirely. From the area of the briefly appearing solid object, a faint stream of near-undetectable particles shot toward Earth, but dissipated long before they could have reached the ground; or so it was thought. What was extremely and unaccountably odd was that later examination of the records showed that the anomaly and the particles associated with it resembled what theorists thought a giant ion propelled spacecraft might look like, a clearly impossible situation.

The occurrence was studied and worried about and tweaked and gone over like an unexpected burst of previously unknown sub-atomic particles appearing in a cyclotron. Despite all the study, little more was learned. Whatever the thing had been, it was gone; gone with the wind, or so it was thought. Almost all of them finally agreed that what they had seen wasn't an object at all, but simply a glitch in the instruments, such as occurred sometimes when sunspot activity was

10

high. Only one person in the department not only held the conviction that they had spotted something material, he noted what he decided was a *direction* the microscopically brief particle stream had taken. None of his colleagues agreed with him; they couldn't see it, and eventually Marco Whitman, a big burly dark haired Italian who looked more like a construction foreman than a scientist, quit mentioning it. He never forgot about it, though. The direction he thought he had seen had been toward Texas. He was a native Texan and hoped to retire back in Texas in the not too distant future. In East Texas, to be exact. He didn't like to think that a bunch of space stuff was preceding him there, but he knew of little he could do about it.

And then it happened again, in reverse.

***

At the same time the low-pressure area formed, and at the same time the problematical stream of odd particles, seen only by their reaction with the atmosphere, headed somewhere (toward East Texas, Marco Whitman thought), a breeding was taking place in Shepherd, a little town about an hour's drive north of Houston. Dora James watched with satisfaction as her pair of miniature dachshunds successfully culminated their tryst, seemingly unaffected by a stream of invisible particles from space which passed through the bodies of the little doggies at just about the same moment. She complimented the little floppy-eared weenie dogs with some treats and smiled, knowing that within a few months she would have another litter of purebred mini-dachshund pups to sell. They would go for two hundred, perhaps two hundred and fifty dollars apiece. For San Jacinto County, not a reservoir of high-income residents by any measure, the prices were pretty steep, but she was sure she would find buyers. She always had before. Miniature dachshunds were in demand, especially the traditional solid red dachshunds such as she was looking at while dollar signs danced happily in her head.

***

When the low-pressure area formed over East Texas, Damon and Beth Stone, a middle-aged couple who lived on a former Christmas tree farm near Shepherd, were grieving. Their mid-sized red dachshund, Biscuit, had hurt his back, a not uncommon occurrence in dachshunds with their excess of vertebrae. They rushed him to see Doctor Bob, their vet, who recommended surgery. Not willing to stint, Damon and

11

Beth sought the best; the small animal surgery clinic at Texas A&M University. Unfortunately, Biscuit developed a rare complication from the back surgery and died a week later.

They brought Biscuit home to the farm and buried him by the garden behind their home where he had spent many happy hours digging for gophers. He was only five years old when he died. The grave was covered and Damon set one of Beth's beautiful handmade and hand-decorated wreaths firmly into the ground on a heavy wire stand to mark Biscuit's final resting place. After that they stood with arms around each other, shedding voluminous tears over Biscuit, a dog so intelligent, so attuned to his people, so happy and so absolutely full of life that Damon had made him the subject of a book, entitled *Doggie Biscuit!*, just ready for publication. At that exact moment the wind rose, blowing dry weeds, pine straw and dried pin oak leaves and bits of debris across the open pasture as if God were paying final tribute to a truly remarkable dog. The wind rose higher, becoming a howling presence that bit through their clothes and carried swirls of dust that brought more tears to their eyes to overlap those from crying over Biscuit's untimely death.

"Let's go, it's going to be pouring in a minute!" Damon said, having to raise his voice to be heard over the gale force winds. He grabbed Beth's hand and they trudged, half running, the fifty yards back to their house, a dwelling that would be a much lonelier place now without Biscuit's presence to lighten it.

Inside, they sat together, not speaking, each of them alone with their thoughts, remembering some special event in Biscuit's life that had brought laugher and happiness to their home. Eventually, they hugged, and sadly, got up to finish the chores for the day. There weren't many. The previous Christmas had been their last with the Choose and Cut Christmas tree farm they had operated the last twenty years. It still seemed strange to Damon and Beth to not be outside working. A farm, even a Christmas tree farm, is never idle, even during the off-season.

***

"It's a likely planet," Exttax remarked after their craft was down and properly stealthed. "It's hardly worth the bother using the Testers."

"Procedure, Exttax," Scout-Leader Fxrrax chided. "Always proper procedure. Get the Testers' kennel and the instruments ready so we can begin at the next sunrise."

Exttax grumbled, but not in thought range of the Scout-Leader. *It's always me he chooses to clean the kennel and service the instruments,* he thought. *And it's me he'll dump the responsibility on if anything goes wrong.* Not that Exttax thought anything would. The protocol for using Testers was so strict, and their genetic character changed enough, so that accidents just didn't happen any more, not since the horrible episode on the planet Rebssttuf, where somehow the Testers had gotten loose. His tendrils quivered at the thought. A whole planet ruined, one that would have been suitable for generations of the race to use. The punishment of the miscreant who had allowed the Testers to escape was legendary, an example for all to think on when handling the creatures.

The Testers had been developed from a little animal native to the home planet, one whose primary defense mechanism was imitation. Selective breeding had been so successful that their powers of duplication had become well nigh perfect, and they were sapient as well now; at least they were once the organism they were imitating reached a certain size. Fortunately, so long as they remained on the home planet, they had no interest in imitation other than as a temporary defense mechanism, and once the danger passed, they always reverted to their original form, where they were only semi-sapient. They kept their numbers low on the home planet as well, like a perfectly behaved domestic animal. If only they didn't have such strong drives when away from home -- but they did.

It was hoped that the last gene reconstruction of the line of Testers used in exploration would prevent such tragedies as happened on the planet Rebssttuf. But of course no one knew yet, and the race hoped they never knew, because who wanted to see something like that happen again if the gene manipulation hadn't worked as they thought it should? No, best to just be careful, especially since the Testers relied on a sensing organ that used quantum powers for communication and imitation, powers that were still only dimly understood.

Despite the potential danger, they were perfect for testing the habitability of a planet when scout ships needed to land and replenish their biomass. Hence their name: Testers. Precautions had been decreed for using Testers after losing that one planet. Only two of their three sexes were ever allowed onto a new planet at one time so that even if by some wild chance the Testers did get loose again, their reproductive drive would be limited (they thought). Without the third sex, they would eventually die off, albeit not without causing a lot of problems if the planet happened to be inhabited by sapient beings, such as this one was.

13

Their homing instinct would decree that they begin the step-by-step process of duplicating the intelligent beings, gaining sapience themselves, along with the ability to build interstellar spaceships and go home. That was definitely not an outcome any of the Twppstt race desired. So far as they knew from their explorations, they had a monopoly on space travel, and they wanted to keep it that way. If the Testers built spaceships in their disguised forms, some of the beings they were mimicking would almost certainly wind up learning to make them too, a horrible thought! The Twppstt race was very xenophobic.

All spaceships carried some testers, especially scout ships such as Exttax served on. Scout ships normally bypassed inhabited planets but this had been a long journey and Fxrrax had decided to stop here to rejuvenate the biomass of the recycling systems.

The Testers weren't normally all that prolific, but if they ever got loose on a new planet, the reproductive drive kicked into higher gear. Given the chance to spread through a new environment, they would, by any means possible, motivated by the homing instinct. Too bad that other dangerous drive couldn't be suppressed as yet, that of one of the sexes being able to disguise their single identifying mark when in the imitation mode, but the specialists were working on it. And in the meantime, extra special precautions were in order.

Exttax was conscientious enough, but he tended to be fearful of the flora and fauna of new planets, a shame he was loath to admit to his fellows. His status was low enough as it was. He made sure the kennel was clean and sterilized, with plenty of trace elements on hand should there not be enough in the immediate vicinity for the Testers to use in their imitative processes. Mostly they simply took advantage of surrounding material, levitating it into their kennel (by quantum exchange, the scientists thought) and that was sufficient, but occasionally some of the rarer elements weren't available close enough for the levitating trick to work.

The little scouting spaceship was well-stealthed when it came through the atmosphere and landed in a pasture, separated from a native dwelling by a narrow line of tall, branched vegetation. Good enough, and the ship remained in the stealth mode while on the ground.

Sunrise came and it was time to see if the biological flora and fauna was compatible with their needs. Exttax very carefully trundled the Tester kennel down the ramp from the spacecraft and onto the soft earth of this so far unnamed planet. The floating beams caused the kennel to wobble a little as they bit at the soft, uneven soil, but he corrected every deviation. The meter ticked off distance until the kennel was far enough from the scout ship that the Testers wouldn't try to levitate objects from inside it once the kennel suppressor fields were turned off and if they needed some element not in the vicinity.

He flicked on his own protective stealth field, then watched the two odd little organisms inside the electrowire cage. Their normal shape of a little six-legged furry animal with three enormous eyes and three small sensing organs on its belly would remain in place until they obtained a gestalt of a living organism from this planet, one near their own size to begin with. If they could duplicate an organism of the planet, then the Twppstt race could live on it if they decided to conquer it later or use its biomass to continue exploring for the present. The testers were perfect at determining that. They were never wrong.

Now all he had to do was hide and wait and pay attention to the recorder. The Testers would not make an imitation of anything if it were watched. In order for the Testers to duplicate a living organism, it first had to come near and then hold still long enough for them to obtain a gestalt, and then hold the form for a sufficient number of time units, without harm, for the test to be a success. Exttax hoped it wouldn't take too long. It would probably depend on the size of the first animal that came near and held still. The larger the animal, the longer it took for the testers to form a pattern of it. He also hoped the tests would be successful and they could reconstitute the biomass needed by the recyclers, otherwise the whole procedure would have to be done again on another planet.

Exttax could only sit silently and patiently on his four legs until some small fauna sample came near, perhaps one of the four limbed creatures with the fluffed out appendage trailing behind which scampered so frantically among the upper branches of the tall growths, up where the brown support columns turned to green. They were probably too active, though. Or perhaps one of the little gray colored creatures that were only a few kitz long. As he waited, his thoughts wandered to the new and exotic tastes of foodstuff they might expect once the biomass here had been declared safe by the Testers.

It might be a long wait, but sooner or later the Testers would get their chance, whenever one of the native animals came close enough, and held still long enough, for them to get a gestalt of it. Even the scientists weren't certain how the testers accomplished that, but it worked, every time. The Testers were semi-sapient in their native form, but knew their role well enough. Of course on this new planet, they would much prefer not to be confined so they had room to scout and gradually progress up the scale of duplication to the large native sophonts and become fully sapient in their form. Then they could multiply that form and try to return home as their genetic makeup decreed.

Unfortunately for them, unless they were loose from the kennel it was impossible to imitate anything but a small animal. And even if out, the small ones came first, then larger and larger ones until they could gain enough brain power to expand their domain; a whole planet of domain in this case. Even then there was a catch. There were only two sexes in the kennel; a third was needed to keep their species healthy and reproductive past a certain time span. Unfortunately (for the Testers), the only place any of that third sex resided was inside the spaceship or on their home planet, and the Twppstt meant to see that they stayed there. However, this pair of Testers contained one of the sexes able to disguise its distinguishing marks when desired, but none of them worried about it. They were only going to test the biomass, then load up with it if it was suitable and depart for other planets.

It was mid-afternoon when one of the scampering creatures Exttax had seen flitting about in the tall vegetation came to ground and landed by the kennel. It swished its bushy hind appendage and looked around while moving in fast, jerky little hops that covered the ground with amazing rapidity. However, it was young and curious and didn't sense any danger. It came right up to the electrowire cage and paused just outside the electrical barrier of the kennel for a few moments, just long enough for one of the Testers to get a gestalt of it. Then it promptly began to imitate the odd little animal. There was plenty of material near the kennel. The proper amount was levitated inside, drawn by the Tester's quantum powers of exchanging atoms of elements; probably through use of its sensing organs, though that was uncertain. The whole process was incredibly fast once it got started. Exttax had hardly blinked his three eyes when the recorder announced it was complete.

Exttax still waited, but he thought it wouldn't be long now. If the duplicate animal the Tester made maintained its new form long enough, the planet would be designated as inhabitable. However, as an extra precaution, the second Tester in the kennel was required to imitate a native form as well. Two examples of the local fauna would do.

It seemed forever before another creature came near. This one was very peculiar. It had no appendages at all, but still managed to move by slithering smoothly along the ground. It paused near the kennel. A thin forked tendril extended from the front end of the animal, waved briefly, then was withdrawn. It stayed still for a moment, basking in a thin ray of a stray sunbeam peeking through the dissipating

16

clouds. Exttax was certain that the other Tester had time to obtain its gestalt, but for some reason it failed.

Curious (and exasperated) Exttax trained an analyzer ray on the creature as it slithered away. He was astounded at its obvious lack of a temperature control mechanism and its feeble brainpower. He had never seen anything like it, but there it was; without a means of controlling its bodily heat, and being nearly brainless besides, the Testers would naturally fail to imitate it. They might be only semi-sapient, but they were smart enough not to go down the scale of sapience so far, especially when the odd creature was so cold.

Exttax wondered how many other species of fauna on the planet displayed the characteristics of the limbless organism. He hoped it wasn't many. He wanted to leave this place, but now he had to wait some more, even though the required amount of time had passed for the first creature. A second successful imitation was necessary according to standard procedure.

At last another little creature wandered by. This one was even smaller than the Testers and had four legs like the one with the bushy appendage, but it sported only a tuft on its rear end and its back legs were much larger than the front. It moved with a peculiar hopping motion. Exttax cared little about how it traveled; he wanted it to stop near the Testers, and he was very pleased when it did. He was even more pleased when the other Tester made a successful imitation. He waited out the required amount of time and was just preparing to recover the kennel, mission successful, when trouble arrived.

It was a big, double horned devil creature that caused the accident. It came along a well-defined trail that Exttax hadn't noticed earlier. It was huge and threatening. Those curved horns alone were sharp enough to rip him to pieces! Exttax backed away, then backed still farther. The horned beast came on, obviously after him. How it saw past his stealth field he had no idea, but he didn't intend to let it get anywhere close to him. He could feel his rear tentacles twitching and trembling with fear, the same fear he took great pains to conceal from his shipmates.

The huge animal suddenly broke into a lope. Exttax screamed through all three orifices and ran, not even watching to see where he was going, other than in a direction opposite the horned beast. He no longer cared who saw how afraid he was.

***

The milk cow heard the feeding bell in the distance and speeded up its pace, not wanting the rest of the herd to eat all the mash before it got to the barn. Unfortunately for the cow, its feet became tangled with Exttax's stealthed kennel. Not only that, the locking mechanism was designed to give a sharp electrical shock to unauthorized beings trying to unfasten it, or even come in contact with it, and the cow was certainly not authorized.

The shock panicked the cow. It tried to back away, but one of its hoofs was hung up in the electrowire of the kennel. If it couldn't see what was entangling its hoof, it could certainly feel, and it didn't like the continuous wave of electrical shocks being administered to its entangled leg. It lowered its head and did its best to grind the invisible obstacle into scrap. When its horns met resistance, it shook its head from side to side, attempting to gore whatever was keeping it from its feeding time and hurting it in the bargain. Since one of its hoofs was still attached to the kennel, something had to give. The kennel surrendered first. The cow's hoof ripped free and its horns flung the kennel over a nearby barbed wire fence and against the trunk of a big pine tree. It smashed solidly into it at just at the right angle to further enlarge the opening made by the cow's hoof. After it came to rest beneath the pine tree, there was no movement in the kennel for a moment, but then the two Testers saw and took advantage of the unexpected opportunity. They wormed their way through the mangled part of the damaged kennel to freedom, leaving it behind and almost hidden from sight near the remains of a fall garden.

The undergrowth beneath the tall vegetation beckoned as a hiding place. Both Testers headed for it without a second thought; escape foremost in their semi-sapient minds. The cow, having vanquished its invisible foe, went on its way, hurrying even faster now, eager for its evening mash and milking.

***

Eventually, Exttax stopped running; or rather, a sweetgum tree stopped him when he looked back with all three eyes to make sure the aggressive beast wasn't following. He ran square into the tree and knocked himself silly. By the time he regained his senses enough to listen, he could no longer hear the sounds of the horned devil creature. Breathing a sigh of relief through two of his orifices, he trudged back toward where he had left the kennel.

Poor Exttax almost died from shock when he found the battered and empty container, no longer stealthed because of the

18

beating the control mechanism had taken. He searched frantically in several directions, but it was far too late. Even if he had seen the Testers, he would no longer have recognized them. Even humans have trouble telling one squirrel from another and few of them took the time to look closely at a rabbit when they were so common.

Exttax was devastated. The Testers were loose; irrevocably and catastrophically loose. It wouldn't even help to use the ship's defensive weapon system to try sterilizing the area. It wasn't designed for that type of destruction. Anyhow, there was no telling how far the Tester imitating the creature with the bushy tail had gone. It knew enough to put some distance between it and the ship. Eventually, Exttax wrapped all but his mobility tendrils around himself and returned to face his punishment, not bothering to gather the remains of the kennel. The castigation he received was so horrible that even the Scout-Leader regurgitated a bit of its last meal before he gave orders to leave the planet, and all its promise, to the Testers.

As for Exttax, he was made to sacrifice a leg, and for the rest of its neutered life would move at the staggering five-legged pace of the criminal class. Even worse, he would see from only two eyes and never know who was behind him, a terrible dilemma in their caste conscious society; so bad, in fact, that he would have terminated his aura had he the means to do so, but even that had been taken from him. He would live the rest of his life with the shame and disparagement of his fellows.

As for the leaders of his race, when word of the accident eventually reached them they began a long debate on whether they should return with a warship and sterilize the planet where the Testers were loose or rely on the changes in procedure made after losing that other planet to resolve the problem. Some trusted the changes to take care of it; they thought the Testers would die out before any damage was done. Others wanted to take no chances since the planet was occupied by sapient beings, regardless of the expense of sending a warship back that long distance. The debate went on and on. A consensus was required for action and none seemed forthcoming. Perhaps none would. The Twppstt were good at procrastination.

***

One of the two Testers which had been in the kennel was injured. It wasn't a fatal wound, but it would take several months to heal. Once the two semi-sapient alien bits of life found each other, they decided that their first objective must be to get away from the immediate area where the huge horned beast had mangled their kennel.

They were appreciative of their freedom, but not enough to want to come close to that thing; at least not until they were strong enough to escape should it attack again.

By the time they decided they had gotten far enough away, the wounded Tester was exhausted. They went to ground in the tree line. By then, it had been dark for hours. They didn't even notice how close to the brick home, surrounded by a barn, pump house and carport, they had come. They probably wouldn't have recognized the edifices as belonging to intelligent beings right away in any case. They were still small and only semi-sapient organisms, not truly intelligent. Their immediate goal was to hide while the injured one healed.

The uninjured Tester dug a hole in the earth large enough to conceal both of them and there they stayed, feeding on microorganisms and tiny bugs while the injured Tester slowly mended. The two animals they had duplicated were part of their group, of course, but they remained above ground and helped protect the injured tester by leading potential predators away from the hiding place and moving about to gain knowledge of the environment. Eventually, they would all go forth, into a world so replete with life and movement that had they been able to express joy, they might have grown legs and danced with ecstatic delight, for on this planet there were no constraints on reproduction, especially when used to try to get back home. The only drawback was the absence of their third sex.

**

For the second day in a row, a sudden and unexpected weather phenomena took place over East Texas, only this time it was a high-pressure area that formed rather than a low-pressure. And for the second day in a row, meteorologists began quietly pulling their hair out and muttering imprecations to the gods of weather at their lack of understanding of how something could blow up so suddenly, with no warning signs whatsoever, and as a further puzzle, be the exact opposite of the one that occurred the day before.

In the Pentagon, Marco Whitman didn't even have to be called in to work; he had never gone home. And again, he insisted something suspicious lurked, no matter how briefly, in the upper stratosphere and near-space environment. The only difference in the two phenomena was that this time, the almost imperceptible shift in the thin clouds riding the air currents at that altitude moved clockwise rather than counter clockwise. Marco went to his superior and suggested that by putting the two phenomena together, it looked to him like something material had entered Earth's atmosphere and then left it, roiling the molecules of air each time with a stream of subatomic particles, all pointed down toward Texas. His theory was dismissed with prejudice. Get on the team, he was told. Don't make waves. He was almost dismissed, along with the phenomena, so for the time being he shut up about it.

2

"I'm suffering from empty lap syndrome," Beth Stone said one day, three and a half months after their beloved dachshund, Biscuit, had died.

It was well past Christmas and she and Damon Stone were relaxing in front of the Franklin stove where a fire was burning, spreading its good bone-warming heat through the room. Damon was dressed in well-worn jeans, flat-heeled boots and a soft old work shirt that had been washed so often the patterns had almost faded away.

Damon and Beth were reminiscing over the designed chaos of the selling season at their Choose and Cut Christmas tree farm, when customers swarmed the place day in and day out, when there was the constant pressure to keep the teenaged boys they hired to help that time of year on the job, and when they were stressed with having to judge how many wreaths they should make and how many hot dogs and hamburger patties might be needed the next day. They also spent half their time looking to the skies, fearing rain, and went to bed each night with aching backs from wrestling with Christmas trees all day. But this had been their last year of operation. They had decided to retire. Beth intended to devote more time to the yard and gardening and Damon wanted to see how he fared as a freelance writer.

With the farm permanently closed now, it seemed odd not to be involved with the winter planting; the hated chore of putting thousands of new seedlings into the ground by hand, regardless of how cold, wet or windy the weather or how much frost covered the ground. Even snow couldn't stop the planting, not that it snowed very often that far south, but it had happened one year.

Damon looked at his wife and brushed a tear from his eye. Biscuit had spent hours and hours asleep in Beth's lap, or even when not asleep he loved to wiggle around and get comfortable there. And when a fire was going in the office, the big room converted from the old two-car garage, Biscuit even preferred her lap to resting on the carpet near the stove.

"I miss him, too," he said, automatically assuming his wife would know he meant Biscuit rather than a dead friend or relative. "We'll never find another dog like Biscuit, though."

Beth turned to her husband, sitting next to her in one of the old battered chairs that had been reupholstered and repaired more often than a snake sheds its skin. "I know," she said gently. "He was our baby." She lifted the tail of her blouse worn loosely outside her slacks and used it to wipe her eyes.

Damon nodded. After the kids were grown and married, they had showered Biscuit with all the love they showed for the kids as they were growing up. Biscuit lived inside the house with them and gradually assumed the status of a people. At least Biscuit had been sure he was a people, and Damon knew he and Beth had treated him like a child and loved him just about as much.

Beth reached over and took Damon's hand in hers and squeezed gently. She said nothing more but simply watched her husband, noting how much more relaxed he was now that the farm was closed and he could spend more time writing, something he loved to do, although so far he hadn't earned much more from his efforts at the keyboard than they had with the Christmas tree farm. The lines in his face softened, making him look younger despite his graying hair, and Beth knew he was remembering something about Biscuit; perhaps the time he had jumped up onto the chair in front of the cash register and rung up three hundred thousand dollars in sales before Damon caught him. Or maybe that time he emptied the precinct office by laying his paws on the pickup truck horn, trying to get her husband to hurry up and finish his business inside.

Damon laughed suddenly, the lines at the edges of his eyes crinkling with mirth. "An empty lap. Yeah, Biscuit never did like to see your lap empty, did he?"

"Of course not -- and he was always in it."

"Well, what do you want? Another dachshund, or maybe try a different breed?"

"You know I wouldn't want anything except a dachshund, and neither would you!"

Damon leaned toward Beth far enough so that their lips could meet. He kissed her, thinking how lucky he had been to meet her, way back when he had still been working in the lab at the county hospital. He loved everything about her, from her short brown hair to her merry brown eyes and her slight, but well-curved frame. Shucks, when she was sitting in his lap, she hardly seemed to weigh more than Biscuit did on the rare occasions when the dog selected his lap over hers. "Well, let's

23

keep an eye out and watch for some miniature dachshund pups for sale."

"Um, I just happened to notice in the paper this morning…"

Damon leaned back and laughed out loud. "You just happened to notice, huh? And then you noticed the empty lap syndrome? Or was it the other way around?"

"Does it matter?"

"Put that way, I guess it doesn't. Go ahead and call and see if they've got any left."

Beth stood up. "I already have. They do."

***

"I have these three left, two females and one male," Dora James said, coming back into her house from outside where the kennels were. She held three little wriggling, squirmy, floppy-eared dachshund pups in her arms.

Damon and Beth stepped closer. All three of the puppies were solid reds, but one wasn't much more than half the size of the other two, and it was a slightly darker color.

Beth eyed the pups with wrinkled brows. She pointed to the littlest one, the male. "He's not from the same litter, is he?"

"Sure he is. He's just the runt."

"But he's so small! Is anything wrong with him?"

"Oh, no! He's perfectly healthy. It's just that way with the runt of the litter; they're small when they're little. He should grow to a normal size, though."

The little male pup whined, the most appealing, heart-rending whine ever whined by a runty little miniature dachshund puppy. If he could have spoken, he couldn't have said it any plainer. *Take me home with you! Please, please take me with you!*

Beth held out her hands. "Come here, little fellow."

She didn't have to say it twice. In a twinkling, the undersized, squirmy little puppy was being held to her breast and trying frantically to get close enough to lick her face. In mere seconds he succeeded, giving her the biggest, wettest, most loving doggie kiss his little puppy heart and tongue could manage. And Beth was lost.

"Here, hold him while I write a check," she said, not even bothering to ask the price.

In more mere seconds the puppy was all over Damon, licking his face and hands and whining with happiness at being held. Damon laughed at the wriggling little bundle, hardly bigger than one of his

24

work-hardened hands. He leaned closer to get a look at the pup's liquid brown eyes. He got his face licked while staring into the depths of those moist puppy eyes and he was lost, too.

***

They had brought a cardboard box to bring their new puppy home in, but he was having none of that. He whined at first and when that brought no results, began crying, *Yi yi yiiiii, please let me out of this old box!*

"Oh well, if he pees on me, I can always change clothes," Damon said, and pulled the puppy out of the box and placed him in his lap. It promptly peed on him out of pure happiness at being out of the box and onto a lap.

***

Behind Damon and Beth's house, a little area of pine straw covered soil shifted, then settled back into immobility. The Testers weren't quite ready to move yet, but the time was getting close. It wouldn't be long now and the two free roaming imitation creatures had gathered such information as their limited intelligence allowed, for once a Tester produced an imitation animal, it was only as intelligent as the original for all that it was truly a Tester.

***

"What are we going to name him?" Beth asked. They were sitting down for breakfast, for once not reading at the table. They often kidded each other about having married the other so they could read at the table without objections. The new member of the household was keeping their attention pretty well occupied at the moment and their books were forgotten.

The little puppy looked up at them, as if knowing they were talking about him.

"He's so little, how about just calling him Little Fellow?"

"I don't like that. He should have a name that suits his personality."

"Such as?"

"Well … Scruffy?" Beth suggested.

"Nah. That's too trite. Besides, he's not a scruffy dog, are you, little fellow?"

25

Yip, the little fellow agreed.

"See?" Damon said. "He's telling you, plain as day, he doesn't want to be named Scruffy."

"Well, how about Piddle? That seems to be his forte."

As if listening, the pup peed on the floor. Fortunately, housebreaking Biscuit had caused them to have the carpeting the house came with removed and hardwood floors put in.

"Ah, now look what you've done, you idiot dog. Come on, outside!" Damon picked up the little dachshund and took him outside and sat him down on the big front porch, intending to watch him and see if he was big enough to negotiate the steps.

The pup took one look at the steps, higher than he was long, and peed on the porch.

"Whoops! None of that, friend! Mama will get you for that!"

Wherf?

"Yes she will, but don't worry. I'll fix it up so you can climb the steps."

Yip, the pup agreed and went over to the old table the cat ate from and peed under it.

Damon laughed. "Ol' buddy, we're going to have to teach you about the great outdoors."

"I heard that," Beth said as she came outside to join them. "You just named him!"

The pup ran over and climbed onto her shoe and began gnawing on the Velcro strap of her tennies.

"What did I name him?"

"Buddy! First you called him friend, then you called him buddy. Let's name him Buddy."

"Aw, that's too trite, just like Scruffy. He..." Like a light bulb coming on over his head as depicted in comic strips, the name hit him. "*Tonto!* That means friend, doesn't it? Let's name him Tonto!"

"Actually, it means 'faithful friend', but that's close enough. Tonto it is."

Damon reached down and picked up the newly named new member of the family. "Come on, Tonto. Let's go inside and see what you like to eat."

***

An hour later, frustrated and irritated, Tonto deigned to eat some bacon, after first turning down Kibbles puppy food, milk, bits of toast, and whatever else Beth could find in the kitchen she thought a puppy might like.

Damon scratched his head. "He's a peculiar little fellow. I never saw a dog so suspicious of his food. It's like he thinks we're trying to sneak some medicine to him in it."

Beth picked Tonto up and held him. "Aw, he's not peculiar, Daddy. He's just getting used to us; that's all."

Tonto reached his little head up and got in a half dozen licks before Beth could get her face out of the way.

"Now if we could just find some nice face-flavored puppy food … anyway, the first thing Monday, I'll make an appointment for a well-puppy check and get his next shots scheduled. Maybe he needs special food or something."

Tonto got in some more face licks. While he was about it, Damon looked more closely at him than he had so far. The end of his muzzle resembled the nose cone of one of the old shuttles. He had long floppy ears that promised to drag the ground if he didn't grow to fit them and brown eyes that … he looked closer.

"Hey, sweetie. Come look. I think our pup may be cross-eyed."

Beth stopped what she was doing quickly; already, she was in the maternal mode. She took Tonto, held him out and examined him closely, despite his squirming. "I can't tell for sure. We'll have to let Dr. Bob have a look."

***

There was little need of that. Later that day, while Damon was sitting in his big easy chair, holding Tonto in his lap and trying to read a book, the pup decided he wanted down. He took a step or two on Damon's legs, then launched himself into the air. Damon looked up just in time to see him doing a perfect imitation of a diver going off the high board. Unfortunately, there was no water waiting on the hardwood floor thirty inches below. Tonto landed squarely on top of his little puppy head. He rolled over and sat up and began howling as if he had cracked his skull in a dozen places.

Damon grabbed him quickly and held him while Beth came rushing in to see what had happened.

"He jumped off the chair while I wasn't watching and landed on his head," Damon said, practically in tears. He was ashamed that his attention had lapsed just long enough for Tonto to leap from the chair and hurt himself.

Beth took the little pup and held him to her breast. He was still howling, although not quite as loud. "We'd better take him in to see Dr. Bob. He might have broken a bone."

"It's the weekend."

"*Oh, Kitty Mess*! They're just like kids, always hurting themselves on weekends when the doctor isn't available."

Tonto's howls tapered off to whimpers and then little snuffling sounds as Beth gently rocked him against her breast. She sat down in her easy chair and petted him while Damon stood beside her chair, feeling as helpless as a man at a bra fitting.

"Why on earth did he jump off the chair?" Beth asked, then remembered. "Oh. Gosh, maybe he does have something wrong with his eyes. Maybe his depth perception is off. We'll just have to watch him."

***

The area of pine straw covering the place where the Testers were hiding while the injured one healed began shifting. A moment later the two Testers emerged, senses alert and ready to assume the shape of any nearby animal should they be threatened. There was nothing around to bother them at the moment.

They began mating, and within a very short time there were three testers where previously there had been two. The original ones were a bit smaller than before, having given up some of their sustenance to make the new Tester. And shortly thereafter, they no longer looked alike. Two returned to the countenance of squirrels they had used when escaping and the other took up the characteristics of a little half grown rabbit it saw nearby.

The three alien creatures left their hiding place and began roaming about. Over the next few weeks their numbers slowly increased, as did the number of earthly animals they duplicated. Those maintaining their normal structure directed the activities of the others through their peculiar sensing organs. The territory they covered increased and the variety of fauna they duplicated also increased, always a species a little larger than before.

There was an opossum and a baby raccoon, but the faux fox was the most intelligent of the creatures, being the largest of the imitation animals. It recognized the brick house as something constructed by intelligent beings native to the planet and urged some of its fellows to explore around the place. At first their primary urge had been to reproduce and expand their domain, but now another

28

imperative was beginning to replace it, that of seeking beings of higher intelligence to duplicate. The imitation fox had as much brainpower as was needed to direct affairs while the Testers retaining the original shape remained hidden. And over all the territory the originals and the imitation earthly animals covered, there was communication through the peculiar little sensory organs even the imitations possessed, although some of those were hidden, depending upon the sex of the individual.

The aliens, in slow fits and starts, moved toward the Stone's house, driven by unconscious needs. Some went astray, or were eaten by predators, but the majority stayed close to where they sensed sapient beings, and close to the originals. The Testers weren't in a great hurry but they were implacable. They moved and reproduced as their peculiar genes dictated, aiming to eventually duplicate the most intelligent of the native fauna, the humans.

First, though, they wanted to spread their numbers widely enough so there wouldn't be any question of stopping them. A few of the smaller imitation animals were ordered to move in closer to the house, but there they were momentarily stopped, stymied by something they had never encountered before.

3

"It's hard to tell just what he sees," Dr. Bob said. "I can tell you that his vision isn't normal. There are specialists who have instruments and ways of finding out but it's very expensive and really not too accurate."

"But what should we do?" Beth asked plaintively. She stroked Tonto's back and let him lick her hand. He was sitting on his haunches on the examining table, not at all afraid. He was interested in the smells and noises of Doctor Bob's Animal Hospital and Clinic.

"Can he get around all right?"

Damon laughed. "He can as long as he doesn't get in too much of a hurry. At first he was bouncing off walls and furniture when he ran through the house, but he's sort of learned."

"But he still has trouble outside," Beth said. "He runs for the porch and tries to jump up on it while he's still three feet away! And when he tries to go down the steps Damon fixed for him, he usually misses the first one and tumbles the rest of the way."

Damon chuckled at the memories. "She's right. He can see, but his perception is off somehow."

Dr. Bob hated to let on that he had no good advice to offer, but he was an honest veterinarian. When he didn't know something, he admitted it. "I think you should just continue to observe him for the time being. You said he manages, after a fashion. I think he'll adjust over time. Now let's see what else we have."

Dr. Bob began his exam with knowing, gentle hands, letting Tonto lick his face first to show he was friendly. "Uh oh," he said presently.

"What's wrong?" Beth and Damon both asked.

"He only has one testicle."

"What! Oh the poor little fellow!" Beth picked him up and hugged him as if it was her husband the doctor was talking about who had only half his vital components. Tonto didn't miss the chance. He

30

saw well enough to get in a few face licks while Beth's face was that close.

"It's not serious," Dr. Bob explained. "At least I don't think so. Normally when you see this sort of thing, the pup actually does have both testicles, but one of them hasn't dropped like it should have. But Tonto only has the one that's visible. However, it shouldn't be a handicap. One should suffice for anything he needs to do." He felt around the dog's groin some more, just to be sure. "Hmm. It is kind of strange, but it's like his eyes. He was just born that way. Something happened at conception that shouldn't have. Maybe a sunspot gave off some ionizing radiation and he was in the way." He shrugged. "Actually, we don't know what causes most oddities like this. But don't worry. He seems like a healthy little fellow. He should do fine. Do you want to have him neutered?"

Damon shuddered, like any typical male at the mention of having the family jewels removed. "I don't know about that," he said, instinctively protective even though it wasn't his reproductive apparatus being talked about.

"Let us think about it," Beth said. "He's still suffering from that knock on the head. And he hates pain. I accidentally stepped on his tail the other day when he got underfoot and he howled for an hour."

A slight exaggeration, but Dr. Bob got the idea. "Sure. There's no hurry. Have you noticed anything else unusual about him?"

Damon and Beth exchanged glances. They had, but didn't know exactly how to describe most of them. Tonto appeared to have a deficit in the food detecting part of his nose. He had to approach food from several angles, looking at it (or trying to) and even when he finally decided it might be edible, he had to peck at it, like a chicken, for several minutes before deciding to eat, and even then, he went at it more like a cat than a dog, taking his time and chewing thoroughly. He acted like he had problems chewing, or perhaps just preferred to savor his food instead of gulping it down like normal dogs. Beth explained that aspect of his behavior.

Dr. Bob examined Tonto's jaw and teeth, manipulating them and his head and neck with his perceptive hands, but could find nothing wrong. Neither could he explain the behavior, as he readily admitted. "Anything else?"

Again Beth and Damon exchanged glances. "Nothing we can put our fingers on right off-hand, but ... well, he doesn't act like he's all that bright."

31

"He's not stupid, though," Beth was quick to come to his defense. "He learned not to bite Velcro too hard when he's playing with him."

"Velcro?"

"The cat. We named him Velcro because he sticks to everything. He stuck to my sweater when I picked him up while we were visiting Damon's brother in Okalahoma and wouldn't let loose until we got back to Texas."

"Sounds like your brother has invented a great way to find homes for kittens," Dr. Bob commented. "Maybe I'll try to learn the technique. We always have a surplus. Now about the behavior, him not being very intelligent. That may be a symptom of being the runt of the litter, but probably it's just a reflection of him not seeing as well as normal dogs do. Watch him until next visit and let's see how he does."

***

"We have a strange dog," Damon remarked a few days later. Tonto lay at his feet panting, completely out of breath. He had just spent the last fifteen minutes charging through the house in a set pattern, from under the table in the office, through the kitchen, behind the stereo, under the side tables beside the two easy chairs, and on to a skidding, sliding turn at the fireplace, then back under the central coffee table, under the two guest chairs, under the dinette set and weaving through the chair legs, back to the kitchen and out to the office, then repeating the pattern again and again until he was utterly exhausted.

"How so?" Beth asked.

"He can't see well enough to keep from bumping his nose when he tries jumping up on the porch or going down the steps, yet he can charge through the house like a loose cannon ball and not hit anything."

"True. But remember how often he bumped his little nose until he learned where everything is?" Beth came over and picked him up, getting her face licked in the process. "He's not so strange. He knows every time when he gets a chance to lick my face and he never passes it up."

"Me either, but you know what I'm talking about. He's got a one-track mind -- and it just doesn't have many tracks. And have you noticed? He can't jump like a normal dog. The best he can do is about six inches."

"It's not that he can't jump; it's just that he doesn't have any depth perception or something like that. He's scared he'll fall. Besides, I don't care. He's ours and I love him."

"I do, too," Damon admitted. "Shucks, who wants a normal dog when you can have a cross-eyed, one-testicled, addle-brained dog with ADHD?"

"Can dogs have ADHD?"

"Kids have it; why not dogs? Or maybe he's a little autistic. You have to admit, he marches to his own drummer. And look at the way he plays outside. You've seen it."

"Yes," Beth admitted. "Although the little fellow concentrates so hard it looks more like work than play. And guess what? He decided he didn't have enough to do and added an extra duty. Now he spends an hour every morning and evening rearranging the hose I use to water the plants. In fact, I just let him out. I bet that's what he's doing now."

Soon after Tonto was big enough to roam about outside on his own, he had begun displaying an odd sort of behavior. Most dogs will play with sticks, but Tonto went to extremes -- and he didn't just play. He worked. He discovered that if he held a stick in his mouth and moved with it, he could push the pine straw on the tarmac of the driveway into piles. It was a compelling sight, watching the small, floppy eared, long bodied dog almost the same color as the pine straw search under the pine trees until he found a stick of the right length to suit him. Then he would grasp the stick in his mouth and hold it straight out in front of him and walk along with his head down and the other end of the stick in the loose pine straw, pushing it up into piles. Once he got the technique down, he spent hours at the task, until the tarmac was covered with little hillocks of shoveled up straw.

They went out to watch and got another surprise in the long line of whoopsies experienced since Tonto came to live with them. He wasn't fixing the hose into the pattern he had decided it belonged in, regardless of Beth's intentions. He had finished that part of his day's work and was getting ready to shovel some straw. They stood at the back door and watched as Tonto searched for a stick of the proper length. He grew increasingly frustrated at not finding one, as if he were late to work and afraid of getting chewed out by the boss. Finally he dragged a dried branch onto the tarmac and began chewing on it, about midway along its length. In a few minutes he had the branch chewed into two pieces, both just about the length he preferred. Happy now, he picked one of them up in his teeth and holding it straight out in front of him, proceeded with his day's work of shoveling straw.

"Did you see that? Now that's truly amazing," Damon said. "I've never heard of *any* animal doing that, much less a dog."

"What's so amazing? He couldn't find the right kind of stick, so he chewed one to the right length."

"Beth, what we just saw was an example of a dog manufacturing a tool for a specific task! Animals may use tools, but they don't make them!"

"So call Gordo and get him to do a paper on Tonto," Beth said with a laugh.

"I may do that," Damon said, shaking his head, still astonished at what they had just seen. "Gordo would love it!"

Gordon Ruttledge was called Gordo by all his friends. They had met Gordo while working overseas right after they married. He was a genius who had once worked for NASA as a xenobiologist, but been fired for bringing his flask to work with him and uncapping it periodically during the day. As Gordo put it, "A little nip now and then keeps the creative juices bubbling. NASA is just too goddamned hidebound to see the advantages of stimulating the brain cells at timed intervals. I showed them figures but those MBAs these days don't understand simple math."

Gordo's calculations weren't understood even by the brightest minds at NASA. Most of them thought he was crazy and wondered how he had ever gotten a job there to begin with. After NASA fired him, he worked as a pharmacist in the Texas prison system for a while, making use of one of his many degrees. He was employed now at the University of Houston as an assistant professor of biology, happily subverting freshmen and doing research no one else even remotely comprehended.

"We'll invite him up one weekend soon. In the meantime, let's go look at the garden. I need to start tilling it before long so you can get your vegetables planted."

"Just a minute, let me put on my shoes."

The "garden" was a forlorn looking remnant of what had been a luxuriant fall growth of potatoes, broccoli, spinach, radishes and a few other vegetables that did well late in the year. Now it was mostly covered with a growth of dried weeds killed by winter frosts, but the rows still stood out plainly, raised a few inches higher than the furrows between them.

Damon had brought a handful of bamboo stakes with him and began pushing them into the well-worked soil, marking off the limits of where he intended to till. He had just pushed one stake into the ground and was rising up when a sparkle of light caught his attention. It was coming from something almost concealed in the brush beneath the big pine tree marking the beginning of the tree line separating the house from the pasture and garden. "I wonder what that is?" he said to Beth, pointing.

Her gaze followed the direction of his extended arm and finger. "Why, I don't know. Look, whatever it is seems to be blinking, like a light or something."

Damon walked over closer to the pine tree in order to get a better look. At first he couldn't comprehend what he was seeing but then it all came into focus. "It looks like a cage of some sort, but I wonder what that blinking light is all about. For that matter I wonder where it came from." He glanced toward the barbed wire fence that separated their property from their nearest neighbor, a good half mile away, thinking briefly that it might be a live trap of some sort set out by one of the renegade trappers in the area, then discarded the idea. Maybe something to do with their neighbor's cows? A cow path bordered the fence for a short distance near the garden before turning into the woods. He discarded that idea, too, as he got closer. A live trap wouldn't have a blinking light on it, or at least none he had ever seen had.

Beth followed along with him and shortly they were standing near the discarded cage. It had been winking its attention light all this time, drawing power from an incredibly efficient little generator built into the kennel. She bent over to see if there was an on or off switch. She reached out and touched part of the electrowire lattice.

"Ouch!" Beth yelped, jerking away. "The damn thing bit me!" She stuck her finger in her mouth and sucked on it.

"Huh? Let me see!"

She took her finger from her mouth and held it out so they could both look. There was no apparent wound. "It felt like an electrical shock." She looked down at the kennel, still winking its light at them. "Maybe that little blinking light was warning us not to touch."

Damon discovered he was still holding a bamboo stake. Beth watched as he cautiously extended it to the kennel and touched it. She let out her pent up breath as nothing happened, then peered closer at the cage. "It looks like something tore its way out of it. See, where the wires are bent there?"

"Uh huh. I think you're right. It would have to be a pretty strong critter, though. This thing isn't that big." He continued exploring the rectangular kennel with the stake and finally used it to tip it over. It seemed to Beth that it took very little effort. That brought another light into view. It was glowing softly in the middle of one of the lengthwise supports to which the wire lattice was attached. He touched it with the end of the stake and pushed. The blinking light went off.

"I wonder if that turned off the electricity," Beth said.

Damon grinned. "Only one way to find out, I guess."

"It'll hurt if it's still live," Beth warned.

"Uh huh, but I guess I can stand it if you could." He closed his eyes and touched a finger to a part of the gridwork. "Nothing. I guess I turned it off, whatever the heck it is."

"What now?"

"I'm going to take it back to the house and fiddle with it in the shop. It's a damn strange looking thing, isn't it?"

Beth had to agree. The supporting columns formed a box about three feet long and eighteen inches of so high and wide. The wires of the grid were about two inches apart in each direction. The whole thing was colored a metallic green. At each corner was a little boxy affair a couple of cubic inches in volume. Some of them had markings that resembled a cross between Chinese pictographs and Arabic writing. There were small raised areas like tiny blocks on the corner boxes. When Damon scratched at the wire with his fingernail. It felt smooth and faintly warm, as if it were still receiving power from somewhere.

He picked up the cage.

"Is it heavy? Do you need any help?" Beth asked.

Damon laughed. "It hardly weighs anything. Lighter than aluminum, even. Isn't it the damnedest thing you ever saw?"

"It sure is. You be careful with it, hear?"

"I will," Damon assured her. "And if I can't figure it out in a few days, I'll call Gordo and get him to come up and see what he thinks."

***

Trying to determine the purpose and working of the abandoned cage distracted Damon from the novel he was writing. He made no progress other than still being able to turn the winking light on and off.

Once Beth had the garden under control, they both decided to take a weekend away from their duties and invite Gordo up for a visit. In the meantime, Tonto's work day had become more sophisticated. He discovered that by finding a downed limb with a flange of leaves or pine straw still attached at one end, he could use it to sweep his pine straw instead of just shoveling it. He held these branches in his mouth

36

sideways and turned in circles, sweeping the loose straw into large piles. He appeared to enjoy that activity, but still shoveled straw with his shorter sticks held in front of him. He'd improved his technique there, too.

He became so confident that he actually began to run with the stick held straight out from his mouth, pushing his straw quicker, a clear indication of him striving for efficiency at work. Seeing him run with the stick in his mouth and the straw piling up in front of it made Damon and Beth both cringe at the thought of the stick catching an obstacle or a crack in the tarmac and jamming the other end down his throat. It never happened, though; somehow he avoided that calamity. Damon swore he had a sixth sense that kept him from it.

But in the meantime, Tonto learned little more. He still wasn't completely housebroken, even though he was old enough now to be cocking his short little leg -- and as often as not, peeing on his chest. Damon did teach him to fetch one squeaky toy, but it was the only one he would do that trick for. He learned to roll over on his back for a belly rub, and like shoveling straw, carried it to extremes. He spent half his time in the house rolling onto his back and happily enticing one or the other into bending over and rubbing his tummy, a feat he performed with no notion his people might have bad backs from farming for so many years. Neither of them minded, though, not when they looked at his happily lolling tongue and wriggling little body or his deep brown eyes that wouldn't stay focused.

***

Gordo dressed just about the same as Damon, in jeans and an old western shirt, for the mild Houston weather had chased the last bit of winter away and spring was in full flower.

Damon and Gordo were easy to tell apart, though. Gordo thought time spent on shaving or getting a haircut was wasteful. When his beard or hair started falling onto the keyboard of his computer or into the can of beer he carried everywhere, he hacked a few inches of it off, but otherwise pretty well ignored it.

The two men shook hands. Gordo's right hand was twisted from an injury in an automobile accident while driving with one too many nips under his belt.

"Hi, Beth," Gordo said, then turned to Damon. "You sumbitch, how come you retired before I did? I thought you were going to run this goddamn farm forever. Now what are the little kids going to do? They'll think Santa Claus retired, too."

37

"Yeah, one of our grandsons asked his dad if there would still be Christmas after Grandpa closed the Christmas tree farm. They'll get over it, though, and I don't miss it a damn bit," Damon said.

"No?"

"Hell no! If you ever froze your hands dipping those damned wreaths in that green goo a dozen times a day, or going out at midnight so a customer could cut a tree because he forgot what our hours were, or growing purple tentacles out your ears from getting into all that pesticide and wrestling with contrary tractors on cold winter mornings, you wouldn't miss it either."

"Huh, guess not. Hell, I'm retiring at the end of the semester myself. I combined some fuzzy logic with chaos theory and the color of the dog food the greyhounds get for breakfast and found out I can beat the odds at the dog races. I made six K last month."

"I'm obviously in the wrong profession," Damon said. "I made six dollars last month writing. Come on in, I've got the Coors cooling."

***

Gordo noticed Tonto after they were inside, and greeted him after he had his hands on a beer, the first thing he always looked for wherever he went. "Well, hello, pup. You're new here. Come see old Gordo and I'll give you a sip of beer."

Tonto cocked his head and eyeballed the hairy apparition with his impaired vision. He approached cautiously, trying to decide if it was human or not. Gordo poured a dollop of cold beer into the palm of his hand and held it out. Tonto sniffed, circled the hand, and sniffed some more.

"Hurry up, dog, or I'll drink it myself."

Tonto touched his nose to the beer, then shook his head. He came back, touched it again, then gave it a lap. And another lap. In a couple of seconds he had Gordo's hand clean.

"Okay, I guess we can be friends now," Gordo said. "But you're a tiny little fellow; you better grow some more before we let you try the hard stuff."

Tonto left Gordo and bumped into the leg of a chair. He backed up then headed for the door. In his little addled doggie mind, it was time to go to work.

"Hey, Gordo, you have to see this," Damon said to their guest. "Our new pup is going to work."

"Work?" Gordo appeared to be horrified. "Poor little fellow, not even grown and already having to carry lunch buckets and punch fucking time clocks. What's the world coming to?"

They followed Tonto toward the back door. Damon opened it and Tonto bounded away, heading for the clear area of the tarmac behind the parked car and trucks.

"Now he's on the job," Damon told Gordo as he closed the door behind them. "You've never seen anything like it."

But instead of working, Tonto began barking, a frenzied torrent of shrill yelps neither Damon nor Beth had ever heard before.

4

Having progressed up the scale of intelligence to the fox, and having increased their numbers somewhat, the Testers were now ready to try for bigger game, meaning access to the dominant species of the planet.

The imitation fox directed the scouting, using one of its members in the guise of a rabbit to move closer to the artificial edifice. Already it had noted the comings and goings of a long bodied, floppy eared creature that apparently lived within the abode of the intelligent species, and was subservient to it. It also noticed that the creature apparently wasn't very intelligent. It spent most of its time outdoors at activities which seemed to have no meaning at all, and paid no attention whatsoever to the local fauna that inhabited the area and frequently came right up to the edges of the area where the intelligent beings lived.

If the Testers could duplicate the smaller creature that was allowed inside, then access to the larger, intelligent ones would probably be assured in that guise, and they would be one step closer on the route back to their home. The Testers had also deduced that the reddish brown animal had definite limits to its territory unless it was in the presence of the large upright sapient species. It was also hoping to catch the animal asleep, or at least holding still for a few moments so it could be duplicated, but this didn't appear to be the Testers' day.

***

"I've never heard him bark like that," Damon exclaimed.

"Oh no! I bet it's a snake!" Beth said, horrified at the thought, remembering how often Biscuit had been bitten for intruding into a copperhead snake's territory. And Tonto had already been bitten twice himself before he got the idea that copperhead snakes were bad business and best left alone. She hurried around the end of their little pickup truck, fully expecting to see Tonto engaged with a serpent even though he had never barked at one before -- or much of anything for

40

that matter. She cleared the truck and stopped abruptly, almost causing her to be run down by the others.

"What's he doing?" Damon asked, edging around his wife and trying to get a better look. He knew their dog had been barking in the area where the electrical fence they had put in to keep him from straying was laid out.

Beth turned her head toward him. "He's barking at a rabbit!" She laughed, relieved that their pet was in no danger. "See? It's just beyond where the electric wire's buried." Tonto would not cross the barrier for fear of getting a shock from his collar that was attuned to the electrical wire but he continued barking furiously at the little rodent, hovering just out of reach.

"What the hell is a rabbit doing out in broad daylight?" Gordo asked. He tilted the can of Coors he had brought along to his mouth. "Have you seen them before?"

"Oh, sure. They hang around the garden and come out in the yard in the mornings and evenings, but I've never seen Tonto bark at them before, or seen one just standing out in the open like this. He's just not interested like most dogs would be, but then he's a strange dog," Damon said. "There's not much telling what he'll do. But this is funny. He usually ignores rabbits, and most other animals for that matter. He does like to eat lizards, though."

Gordo frowned. Damon could almost see his brain cells dancing behind his forehead. Anything out of the ordinary always intrigued him, and a dog barking at a rabbit which was out in broad daylight and which apparently knew that Tonto couldn't cross the pet fence certainly wasn't normal. "Let's go see."

They walked toward Tonto, who was still yelping frantically and dancing around in front of the rabbit at the edge of the driveway. It looked like a perfectly ordinary small rabbit, just like any other they could see around the place most mornings or evenings with no trouble at all. They hadn't tried to eliminate them because they were cute, and in any event, Velcro the cat kept them pretty much under control when the larger predators were lax in their duties.

As the humans approached, the barking became even more passionate. Tonto began interspersing his barks with snarls and growls as if the rabbit was a mortal enemy and he was desperately hoping it would cross the barrier so he could get at it.

Damon got close enough so that he could lean forward to examine the rabbit closer. When he did so, Tonto turned and barked at him, obviously trying to warn him away. Damon straightened up and edged closer.

Tonto was having none of it. He knew that the human he owned was in dire danger and he had to protect him. He gave Damon a warning bark, trying to tell him to stay clear, then he attacked, accepting the punishment of the electrical shock he knew he would get. He yelped in agony as he passed the wire, then he was clear.

There was a blur of Tonto in motion amidst flying pine straw and then he had the rabbit in his mouth in a death grip. He shook it violently, trying to break its neck, then flipped it into the air. When it landed, it tried feebly to run, but Tonto dove at it again, this time catching it by the neck instead of the middle. There was an audible crunching noise. The rabbit twisted and vibrated while Tonto held on. He shook it again, vigorously, then its motion died. Tonto dropped it onto the tarmac and began circling it, making sure it was dead. Finally he touched it with his nose, gave it a few shoves, then cocked his head as if listening to a death rattle audible only to himself. Satisfied, he left it lying and started to come over to Damon. He stopped as he remembered the shock he would get if he crossed that invisible barrier.

Damon carried an activation switch for the pet fence on his key chain. He quickly switched the electricity off then said, "Off, Tonto," the signal which the little dachshund had learned meant the electrical barrier was stilled for a moment. He ran to his people once he heard the magic words. "On, Tonto," Damon told him as he thumbed the switch again, letting him know the electricity was once again active.

While Damon and Beth were petting Tonto and soothing his ruffled fur and telling him what a good doggie he was for protecting them, Gordo ignored the dog and picked up the rabbit. It looked more or less like any other he had ever seen, and just like the ones he had kept as a pet and played with as a kid. He started to throw it away, then reconsidered. He took his reading glasses which dangled from a chain around his neck so he could keep up with them when he was drinking, which was almost always, and put them on. He scrutinized the animal closely, squinting his eyes as he peered at it.

"Hey, troops, have a look."

The others gathered around Gordo. He showed them what he had discovered. "Something doesn't compute here. This ain't no regular rabbit; the goddamned thing is growing jewels on its belly. We'd never have noticed except your dog took care of it. He obviously sensed an intruder on company territory, and since you don't employ security guards, he took care of the problem himself."

"Don't be silly, Gordo," Beth said. "Jewels on a rabbit? You've had too much beer."

"I haven't even had a half a case today yet, not to mention that it's impossible to have too much. Too little maybe, but not too much. And this little fucker does have jewels, I shit you not. See?" He pointed to the upended rabbit cupped in his hand. Three tiny glittering, faceted jewels arranged in a triangular pattern adorned the dead animal's belly, large enough to be clearly seen in the fur. "What I want to know is why the little bastard thought it had to disguise itself as a regular rabbit when it's obviously something different. It's like it was a spy or an alien in enemy territory or … alien? Be goddamned. I bet…"

Damon watched fondly as his friend's mind went into its super-genius mode. Gordo's brain cells didn't follow a linear path; their wiring was as twisted as a willow sapling after a tornado. He jumped to conclusions before most people even knew there was a problem. "Gordo, if you think something's awry, bring that thing with you and let's go inside and get some new canned attitude. We need to cogitate about this." Despite thinking the jewels on the rabbit's belly were probably a strange fungus or a wound where leaking serum had crystallized, he had a vague notion of impending disaster. Gordo was seldom wrong when he jumped to conclusions, bypassing the chains of logic normal people had to contend with.

"Goddamned right. Canned attitude it is, with maybe a little Jack Daniels or Jamesons for flavoring."

As they left, Tonto went back to work, satisfied that all was well again within his domain. Except for the damned water hose. The humans had moved it out of place again while he was protecting them from the intruder and it was no longer arranged properly. He spent half an hour dragging and tugging until it was in the positional pattern that his odd little doggie mind had decided was its proper place in the great scheme of things, then returned to shoveling straw. It had been windy the previous day; there was lots of work to do.

***

Gordo set the ersatz rabbit down on a napkin on the coffee table in the den. Beth brought them each a cold beer, then busied herself with making frozen pina coladas from a bottle of Bacardi rum.

"Damn, wish I had a good microscope here so I could look at this critter's innards and those little jewels in more detail," Gordo said. He leaned forward from the couch where they were sitting and nudged it with his forefinger. "Guess it's dead now, or maybe playing possum."

"I doubt it could slip that over on Tonto. He may not have but two brain cells, but he knows when something's dead all right. I think."

43

Gordo chugged down half his beer. "Tell me more about your dog. Tonto, you said? What does he do other than chase rabbits?" Gordo's brain was still buzzing. He loved puzzles.

"There's not much to tell, Gordo, but he doesn't chase rabbits or any other animal and never has until today. About all he does is work with sticks and straw. And water hoses now, since he took on that part time job." Damon picked up the dead rabbit and examined it in a cursory manner, trying to figure out why whatever kind of animal it was made Tonto think it was so dangerous. As he turned it around in his hand, the overhead lights caused parts of its belly to glitter. The three tiny jewel-like spots winked at him, like a tiny three-bulb signal light. "Hey, Gordo. Take a look." He pointed to the sparkling dots, each a deep blue-red color.

Gordo took out his reading glasses and scrutinized the spots. They were still arranged in a triangular pattern. "Huh. Now they're blinking at us. Wonder what those are? Eyes? Brains? Balls? Tits? Spending money? Whatever, they had to have had a function. Or hell, maybe they still do, even if the thing's dead. We need a stereoscope." As he spoke, the internal light from the three little jewels faded away and the blinking ceased.

"I don't have a stereoscope handy, but you can take this back with you and look at it on campus. I wonder if those little spots are what made Tonto get on to it? Nah, he can't see that well. But he sure spotted it as an odd duck right quick, didn't he?"

"Helluva dog, I'll grant you that. Tell me more about him."

Damon began relating Tonto's peculiarities. Beth joined him and filled in anything he forgot, including his age.

Gordo's brain cells went into overdrive again at the mention of his age. He tilted his beer and drained half of it to give them more of an impetus, then jolted them again with big gulps of his cold pina colada. "He got his genes scrambled at conception, that's what happened. Some ions from that crazy weather pattern fits the time scale, anyway. It sounds like he's the doggie equivalent of a human with Asperger's syndrome, plus some mixed up wiring causing his visual problems -- if they are problems." He thought for a moment. "Hmm. I wonder..." He did some mental calculations and eyed Tonto again, remembering rumors from the Pentagon, where he still had connections despite having been fired from there too, when a general caught him with one hand up a WAC captain's skirt and the other hand holding a bottle of Jack Daniels.

Damon could practically see his brain racing, connecting extremely unlikely occurrences into an equally unlikely scenario.

44

Beth frowned. "Scrambled genes at conception? Why would they not be problems?"

Gordo shrugged. "Maybe that's what turned him on to this weird rabbit; he saw it differently than you or I or another dog would have. And you said he acts like he has problems smelling, like with his food. Maybe he just smells in a different way than normal dogs. Goddamn, I'd like to take him to the lab with me and see what his innards are like too. I'm just speculating, but there really could be a connection with that weather pattern that happened a few months ago."

Damon and Beth simultaneously remembered the two disturbances a day apart. Damon chuckled. "I doubt he could possibly be connected to those storms. Heck, he was just being conceived around that time and..." Then he made the connection that Gordo had. He looked at Beth and saw that she had done the same thing.

Beth didn't want to believe anything was *that* different about Tonto, their addled little weenie dog. She looked troubled. "But Gordo, the vet has examined him fourteen ways from Sunday and the only obvious defect is just having one testicle. We're almost certain he's cross-eyed, too, but we didn't spend the money to find out for sure since they can't do much about it anyway. Besides, as long as he has pine straw to sweep and sticks to sweep it with, he's happy. So why bother?"

"A one-balled wonder dog. Damon, you better guard him real close; he may be the only creature on Earth who can sniff out the aliens."

"Whoa! Aliens? Like from outer space?"

"Yeah. That's what I said. And notice I said it in fucking plural. Invaders don't usually try to conquer a world with one individual."

"Wait a minute, Gordo; you're moving a little fast for me. How can you deduce an alien invasion from one oddball little rabbit that annoyed an addled little weenie dog? I always pictured an alien invasion as a horde of spaceships and millions of little green gremlins running around shooting the men, raping the women and setting fire to wheat fields so we starve to death."

"Yeah, that's how most people think of it. But I doubt aliens will follow our fucking script; most likely any goddamned invasion would be one we'd barely fucking recognize ... shit. I was just speculating; now I've convinced even me, what with that cage or kennel or whatever the fuck it is you told me about. I want to look at it too."

"Can you guys stall off the invasion long enough to get the grill going for steaks?" Beth asked.

"Yup. C'mon, Gordo. Let's go start a fire and do some serious porch sitting."

They took their beers outside and were just in time to see Tonto finish rearranging the water hose. He looked up toward the porch as if to say, *Now leave it like that, okay?*, and headed back to the driveway to begin the serious day's work with sticks and straw.

***

The steaks were grilled to perfection even though Damon and Gordo were beginning to wobble a bit by the time they were done. Then the meal sobered them up some.

While Beth began cleaning up, she handed Damon the bones. "Here, take these out to Tonto. It's about time for him to clock out anyway."

Gordo followed Damon toward the back door. Just as they opened it, Tonto went into the same frenzied barking mode that had begun the visit. They exchanged glances and went to look.

This time Tonto didn't hesitate quite so long before attacking, and this time it wasn't a rabbit; it was a rat, and a big one at that. Tonto would ordinarily have steered well clear of it, having been bitten as a puppy when a blurred visage had aroused his curiosity and wound up nipping his tender little nose. Even his twisted brain cells could associate pain with the object inflicting it and even knowing all that, he braved both the pet fence and the possibility of a painful bite in order to attack. After he had properly disposed of the rat in a furious dancing fight where he somehow avoided its teeth, he left it to the men and began sniffing and pecking at the T-bones to see if they met his standards for consumption.

As he was doing that, and drawing bewildered stares from Gordo, who had never seen a dog so persnickety about a bone, Damon gingerly picked up the dead rat. It was as limp as the rabbit had been after its demise. He handed it to Gordo. "What do you think?"

Gordo looked at it, turned it over, then put on his reading glasses. He peered closely at the rat, examining it critically again. On its belly, three tiny blue-red jewels sparkled in the sunlight. They began blinking. He looked at Damon, then to the heavens.

"Houston, we have a problem."

5

Three days later, Gordo called early in the morning and began talking without any preliminaries. "Damon, have you found any more of those motherfucking imitation rats or rabbits?"

Damon eyed the spare table in the mud room entrance to the office, a big space converted from the garage. It contained a small portable refrigerator which was ordinarily empty but now contained an array of two rabbits, a rat, a small raccoon and an opossum. "Yeah, and that's not all. Whatever it is has graduated to raccoons and possums. I'm keeping them in a little cooler right now, but if you want to study them, you'd better hurry. Beth isn't very happy about my storage spot. And get this, Gordo --" He paused for a moment before relating a painful memory. "I had to shoot Velcro the cat. Or rather I had to shoot *two* Velcros because yesterday morning there was two of him and I couldn't tell the difference because neither of them had those jewels on the belly."

"Hot diggedy damn! Damon, ol' buddy, you're going to have company for a while. I'm bringing a trailer and staying a while, along with a couple of freshmen assistants, a couple of postdocs and a gofer or two. It's definitely aliens, especially considering your cat -- or cats. Besides, that cage you found may look simple but it's so high tech I haven't gotten a handle on it yet."

That made Damon really take notice. If there was a mechanical device in existence that Gordo couldn't determine what wound its clock after three days of study, it definitely made him worry. "You don't have to stay in a trailer, Gordo."

"Wasn't planning on it. It's for my assistants. I can't stand fucking freshmen for long, even if they are female. I figured you wouldn't mind loaning me your other bedroom while I figure this situation out."

"You've got the bedroom, and I sure as hell hope you can tell me what's going on. Poor Tonto is getting tired of all these three-eyed aliens from outer space. They're playing hell with a poor working doggie's routine. And Beth cried all morning after I had to dispose of the cat. She only stopped when I told her what might have happened if he had been an inside cat."

"Yeah, and those three-eyed aliens we're talking about when we see the jewels are probably not even eyes. I think the jewels are for communication of some sort, or maybe some crazy quantum manipulation these critters can do. Anyway, we'll be there tomorrow. How 'bout arranging for the Coors people in the area to make deliveries so I won't have to be running to the store all the time?"

"I'll make sure you have plenty. And hey, I've done a little observing myself. Did you know I keep seeing a fox hanging around in the brush? Normally you rarely see a fox. They're reclusive and stay away from people. And one more thing. After Velcro, Beth got worried about your aliens, so I put up a little fence a few yards further out than the buried pet fence and I keep a mild, continuous electrical charge running through it. Those critters apparently won't cross it, even though Tonto will if he senses one of those things nearby. He just grits his teeth and takes the shock from the pet fence if I don't come quick and deactivate it, but there's not enough juice in the other one to bother him. It sure stops those other outer space varmints, though."

"Good God. They must be goddamned sensitive to electricity. That calls for some sour mash, too. This may require some extra hard thinking. Don't worry about the crew; they can fend for themselves. Goddamn, is this going to be fun! Oh yeah -- if you could live-trap a few of those critters, it would be helpful."

"Live-trap? Hell, Gordo, what do I use for bait? I don't know what they eat -- or even if they do eat. I wish you'd said something before I shot the cats. I might could have gotten them in a cage."

"Oh, yeah. I guess I'm getting ahead of myself. Well, do what you can. See you tomorrow. We oughta be able to whip this little invasion in a week or two."

Damon wasn't nearly that confident and suspected Gordo was whistling in the dark himself. He knew he wasn't nearly as smart as Gordo, but he hadn't fallen off a hay wagon lately, either, and he had been thinking about the imitations. So far as he could see, the invasion would be well-nigh impossible to stop without Tonto, and if it progressed much further, the poor dog would run out of steam just trying to keep the imitators off his driveway, much less out of the woods and house ... house? Whoops. Better not mention that one to Beth, even if the critters wouldn't cross the one strand fence he had erected with the little bit of juice in it. The cat was bad enough, but if she thought a swarm of aliens was trying to get inside, she'd probably insist they move out.

***

Bright and early the next morning Gordo and his trailer pulled into the farm. The travel trailer Damon had been envisioning proved to be an eighteen by eighty-foot monster which had to be brought through the fields since it was wider than one of the culverts. Gordo himself came in his battered old blue van that he drove when he went on field trips. He kept the passenger seat filled with beer, and tossed the empties over his shoulder after draining them. Periodically, he opened the rear door of the van and raked it out to make room for more cans.

Tonto saw the monster trailer being pulled past the house and into the pasture right behind the tree line. Never very brave, he gave a couple of barks and when the monster didn't even slow down, abandoned the pile of straw he was shoveling and ran for the house. When Beth answered his frantic scratching at the back door he scampered in and rolled onto his back, wanting to be picked up. He was shivering by the time she cuddled him to her chest. Part of it was an act, but he definitely didn't like anything bigger than himself that made loud noises.

"He sure doesn't look like an alien sniffer-outer right now," Damon said.

"It's the trailer. He'll be okay once it's parked and he gets used to it."

"He'd better. I can't see us going out every morning and turning over every critter on the premises to see if they've got jewels on their bottom, even if they'd hold still for it."

"I wonder how he spots them so easily?"

Damon shrugged. Tonto did lots of strange things.

***

The trailer and the cars Gordo's crew had followed in were parked behind the tree line, almost exactly where the spaceship had landed months ago. Damon went outside and greeted Gordo as he came from behind the cluster of trees. He was holding a Coors in one hand and a leash in another, to which was attached two dogs, another miniature dachshund and a Chihuahua.

49

Tonto sensed intruders of his own species and began growling and barking from the safety of Beth's arms behind the big bay window of the office.

"What the hell did you bring dogs for?" Damon asked.

"Controls," Gordo said. "We have to find out if Tonto is unique or whether just any dog can sniff out the imitations. These little fuckers are the best I could come up with on short notice."

"They look familiar."

"They should; you saw them at my next door neighbor's place last time you were there. I stole them while she was out shopping."

"Why did you have to steal them?"

"You kidding? She wouldn't risk her little darlings around aliens! Besides, she thinks I'm making alcoholics of them as it is, just because I give them a little nip or two through the fence when I'm outside."

The office door opened and Tonto came rushing out. Knowing Damon would protect him if he got in over his head, he promptly bit the bigger dachshund on its testicles, figuring if he had only one the other dog could function that way, too. After that, he then rolled the little Chihuahua on its back.

The other dogs, having been babied until they were more cowardly than Tonto, quickly allowed him to establish his dominance. Tonto strutted around bravely for a minute or two, then his little tail shot straight out behind him. His ears jerked as they tried to come to attention; unfortunately they were boneless and still dragged on the ground. He gave them a good shaking, disgusted at their inertness, and ran to the edge of the woods behind the carport and began barking.

"Goddamn good deal!" Gordo shouted and yanked his pair of dogs along as he followed Tonto.

The barking was centered on a squirrel looking safely down at Tonto from half dozen feet up the trunk of an oak tree. Gordo got the other dogs to the vicinity. They peed on a bush and ignored the squirrel.

"Stupid little shits," Gordo said. "They aren't worth feeding. Oughta shoot the silly bastards and grind 'em up for cat food."

Damon, who was carrying his .22 revolver again, plugged the squirrel, momentarily quieting Tonto, who ambled back toward the house, intending to get the garden hose positioned correctly so he could begin his main day's work of shoveling straw.

Gordo examined the squirrel with his bifocals. "By damn and by God, there they are. Same little fucking jewels." He pointed them out to Damon, who only nodded. He had a freezer full of varmints with the three little jewels implanted in them already, and a couple without a sign of the jewels.

Gordo put two fingers to his mouth and gave an ear-splitting whistle that startled Tonto so badly he bit through the water hose and sprayed himself in the face. He looked stupidly at the jet of water, tried a couple of times to get a drink from it without success, then proceeded to ignore it while he positioned the hose, soaking himself in the process.

Two well trained freshmen biology majors, both female, came running at the sound of Gordo's whistle. He tossed the squirrel to the nearest of the pair.

"Eeeek!" She screamed and batted it fifty feet into the air.

"Goddamnit, Junie Mae, you grab that critter or back to school you go. That's a *scientific* specimen."

"Well, why didn't you say so?" Junie Mae pouted. She approached the dead squirrel, toed it with the tip of her tennis shoe then picked it up, acting as if she were sacrificing her virginity to the gods of science.

"Don't be so fucking ladylike, Junie Mae. Hold it like you would a hard dick and come along."

The other freshman co-ed snickered.

"What's the matter with you, Ruthie June? You never heard the term before?"

"You're crude, Dr. Ruttledge."

Her companion nodded. The two young women looked so much alike they could have been twins. Both had large breasts and wide hips and wore their hair gathered behind their necks and tied with scarves.

Apparently they were so low on the university food chain as to be unworthy of introduction; either that or Gordo simply forgot. He pretended that he hated having them around, an attitude which only made the co-eds think he was attractive and sexy. It was one problem Gordo had never been able to figure out.

"Come on in, ladies," Damon said. "I'm Damon Stone. My wife's name is Beth."

"Ladies? Goddamned, you'll get them to where they won't handle a squirrel or a dick either, you keep calling them ladies. Where's the beer?"

Inside the house, Gordo loaded the two co-eds up with Damon's specimens from the little cooler and sent them back to the trailer with detailed instructions for his other assistant and the two postdocs. "You'll meet them later," Gordo said. "Right now I want

51

them to get busy making comparisons and preparing slides for me to look at. You got the beer cold?"

It was a little past eight in the morning, but that was late for Gordo. Shrugging, Damon gave him one and took another for himself.

Once loaded for work, Gordo looked around the den. "Did you get me any live specimens?"

Damon grinned. "Yeah, but just one, and Beth made me put it in the pump house. C'mon and I'll show you."

The pump house was located out the front door and around the corner opposite the driveway. "I got you another baby rabbit. It's a little bit mangled. Tonto chewed on its ears while I was rigging a little electric fence and transferring it, probably trying to see what makes them stand up. I think he's jealous because his ears are so floppy. Anyway, I fixed the fence just in case it gnawed its way out of the plastic milk jug I put it in. I punched some holes in the jug, so it should be fine." Damon opened the pump house door and flicked on the light.

"Where -- oh, I see."

Damon stood stock-still. "I didn't have but one specimen."

Gordo looked at him then back down at the jug, now containing at least three little rabbits; it was hard to tell. And it appeared as if the jug had sunk about two inches into the concrete of the floor. He leaned over and started to pick it up.

Damon grabbed his arm. "Gordo, maybe you better be a little careful. Those goddamn things have eaten a hole in the concrete!"

"Huh." Gordo tilted his beer and drained it to get his brain cells in higher gear. He stared back down at the jug and ran his fingers through his scraggly beard and hair. "Looks like they sucked the substance of the concrete up through the holes you cut in the jugs and used it to create the duplicates." He squinted. "Or maybe they ate the bottom out of the jug. Now that's getting goddamned hairy. I figured they must use compost and organic shit and dirt to duplicate, but looks like just about anything will serve. Shit, NASA is going to go crazy. Teach the fuckers to fire me!"

Then he frowned and began wondering why they hadn't just used the whole milk carton, too. He bent to pick it up then saw what had happened. The bottom of the milk carton was gone. Gordo hastily set the top portion back down into the depression in the concrete, again confining the rabbits. Temporarily, he was sure, but maybe the duplicates, which would probably be quadruplicates by the time they returned, would at least stay in the pump house. The electrical barrier Damon had rigged around the jug ought to see to that.

52

By the end of the day, Damon and Gordo were still on their feet, but wobbly. Damon had quit trying to keep up with Gordo's beer derby somewhere around noon, at the specific and direct suggestion of his wife, who by this time was looking almost as addled as Tonto. She had spent part of the day trying to cook and part riding herd on the little dachshund, which had interrupted his work with pine straw on a half dozen occasions to alert his mistress that the invaders were still coming at them.

Tonto was now asleep on his bed with all four feet up in the air, totally exhausted.

"You know, he's actually learning," Damon remarked. "Now he doesn't try to kill the imitators; he just points them out to us and goes on about his business. It's a good thing, too. The poor little fellow would run himself ragged otherwise. Have another hamburger, Gordo. You need to eat more."

"Yeah, you're right. Meat has more protein than beer. I can see my brain cells are going to need to be refreshed both ways. Them goddamned imitators are driving me crazy and this is still my first day with them." He stared into space for a moment. "You know, it just occurred to me, there must be some of the original invaders around here somewhere. I wonder why we haven't seen any of them? Probably small and odd looking, so we'd stomp on them if we got a chance," he said, answering his own question, but then asking himself another. "However, that brings up the question of how far they can be and still communicate with their proxies. Shit. Aliens can ruin a fellow's day, can't they?"

"They sure can," Beth agreed. "What have you found out?"

"Hmm. Well, for one thing, it's dangerous to keep live specimens in the trailer. Those goddamn stupid freshmen went off to smell your goddamned roses and by the time they got back the rabbits had multiplied again by eating their cage. The stupid fucking postdoc fixed me up an electric cage, then the dumb fucker forgot to plug it in. The rabbits were running around all over the damned specimen room."

"How come they didn't eat the jug I had them in?" Damon asked.

"They would have, given a little more time, and they did eat the bottom out of it, if you recall. Remember the box we put them in when I took them from the pump house? They ate it while making more duplicates. Well, they didn't really eat it. They were swapping atoms and molecules by some sort of quantum process, I think, which is also what

I think those jewels are for partly, besides communication. Anyway, after they decomposed the box, I had the postdoc fix up the electric cage, for all the good it did. That's another thing I've learned. They can learn, and the jewels keep on doing something after the critters die for a little while. Maybe telling the others what's happened to them."

Damon shook his head. Gordo's convoluted reasoning and explanations were famous for driving other professors crazy. For some reason, freshmen understood him occasionally, which is why he kept them around. "So where do you have them now?"

"Back in the cage, but now it's turned on. I've got them building some more cages. That one is awfully crowded."

"I think you better put a fence up around your trailer, Gordo."

"Already working on it, or at least the co-eds are. Maybe it'll keep their minds off sex long enough for us to get more work done. We'll just have to watch that nothing comes through when the gate's open to go in and out. I'll get the school to pay for all this shit if I have to twist some tightwad accountant's nuts off. In the meantime, there's another curious thing about the little fuckers. It's goddamned impossible to tell the difference between an imitator and original, even under a microscope. The only way is by the jewels, which I still don't know about. I need to examine them with an electron or tunneling microscope. Down at those magnifications, we might see exactly what they're made of and how they work, but I'll bet even then we won't know what the fuck they mean. Other than they sure didn't originate on Earth. And that brings up the biggest fucking problem so far. Some of the duplicates don't have the jewels on their bellies."

That got a reaction. Damon chugged at his drink. "You mean we may not be able to tell even by the jewels -- or the lack of them -- whether or not a creature is an alien or not?"

"That's the goddamned fucking crux of the matter, all right. I think they still have the jewels but they're concealed in another dimension or some kind of quantum shit like that. Anyway, it's gonna cause trouble, wait and see."

"Are you sure they're aliens? Maybe some naturals got mixed up with them."

"Nope. No chance. I can't see wild rabbits sneaking into a trailer, can you? Besides, Tonto says they're fucking aliens and he's the expert."

Beth and Damon ignored Gordo's profanity with good grace. He used it like a second language and could no more control it than he could resist a cold beer on a hot day. His co-eds thought it was cute. The Dean of Biology thought it was vulgar but he couldn't fire him because Gordo had tenure and besides, he threw ideas out like a volcano spewing rocks and lava for anyone handy to pick up and use once they cooled. Understanding them was a different matter, though. Gordo's ideas were so controversial and incomprehensible to most other professors that they thought he was crazy. The Dean knew he wasn't and hoped one day to gain fame and fortune by stealing an idea he could understand.

"So what's your next step?" Damon asked.

"Next step? Hell, I'm not sure we've taken the first one yet. But I do still have a few contacts at the Pentagon. I'm gonna call and have them send me someone who's real good with computers."

"What for?"

"Because I've got a theory of how Tonto's able to do his thing even if I don't know much about the critters he spots for us. I know a guy who might can help."

Damon was about to ask what his theory was but Beth beat him to the draw, asking a different question. "You know that electrified fence around our place and the one around the trailer you brought that you guys are saying will stop the imitations from spreading?"

"Yeah? What about it?" Gordo asked as he tossed an empty can over his shoulder without looking. It landed in the trash can, dead center.

"Well, I was just wondering. What happens if they imitate a bird?"

Gordo was wrong footed. He stared at Beth then shook his head. "I hate goddamn smart ass broads."

As it turned out, no imitation birds were ever discovered because the Testers were afraid of heights. They came from a high gravity world.

**

"Send Whitman. That wild man upsets everyone around here with his off the wall theories," General Blunderous, called Blunder Ass by the enlisted men, ordered.

"Yes, sir," the Command Sgt. Major of the Pentagon meteorological office said. "You realize, sir, he's our best computer man. He's just been assigned to meteorology because he pissed off, uh, I mean, aggravated Colonel Brevity."

"I know that, but get him out of here anyway. Goddamn bastard wouldn't take a commission so I could court martial his ass. He didn't aggravate the colonel. He beat the shit out of him."

"Yes, sir," the Sgt. Major said sadly. *And there goes the only person around here with a lick of sense*, he thought.

***

"Texas? Why the fuck am I being sent to Texas?" Marco Whitman asked the army clerk, a PFC who spent more time checking her complexion and makeup in a mirror than she did handling reassignments, and her wording on the orders she typed up left lots of room for interpretation.

"I don't know, Dr. Whitman. Here's your orders." She handed him a sheaf of papers and went back to admiring her image in the hand mirror she always kept handy.

Whitman took the documents with bad grace, wondering how in hell he had ever gotten hooked up with the Pentagon in the first place. Probably because of their big bad computers, he thought, better than any university could afford. He bumbled out the door and headed back toward his office, reading his orders on the way.

By the time he arrived, he was smiling. That cute little PFC had inadvertently bollixed the language so much that he now had more power than the general, so long as he used it at his new assignment. And she had given him an unlimited budget. The general had signed off on the orders anyway, since he hated to admit he couldn't interpret a PFC's wording. And best of all, he would be out of the Pentagon.

6

Gordo was up early the next morning with Damon, who still hadn't gotten used to being retired; his body insisted on rising with the roosters. Damon brought big mugs of coffee into the den, thinking how nice it was not to have to drink it on a stupid tractor in the cold or heat or wind or rain.

Gordo took a couple of sips of his coffee then got up and brought a fifth of Damon's Jameson Irish Whiskey back to the coffee table. He added a dollop to his coffee and raised his brows at Damon.

Damon thought a second or two. "What the hell; I'm retired. Besides, we're being invaded by aliens from outer space. That calls for coffee in your whiskey in the morning any day."

"Right on. Except for the goddamned invasion part. I don't fucking get it. If this is an intentional invasion, the motherfucking aliens haven't got any more sense than your dog."

"Tonto isn't that dumb."

"Any dog that goes out and works all day when it could be inside loafing ain't very smart either."

"Good thing he's here, though, or we'd be up shit creek without a paddle."

"You're right," Gordo conceded. "Which reminds me. I'm going to call a few friends. We need to get some sperm from Tonto right away and start breeding more dogs like him."

"What for?"

"Don't be dense. Put some more whiskey in your coffee. What do we do if something happens to Tonto?"

Damon rubbed his unshaven chin. "Yeah. Well, make sure it's a damned good vet. Tonto doesn't like pain."

Gordo sipped appreciatively at his well-laced coffee. He glanced out the big window in the den and spotted headlights. "I see my crew is right on time this morning."

The headlights of cars coming in stimulated Damon's mind more than the jigger of Irish whiskey in his coffee had. "Gordo, what happens if those critters imitate something that gets carried off the farm? Or flies off, like Beth said?"

"Then we've got another goddamned hot spot. One more reason to get some more dogs like Tonto. By the way, I tried those useless little shits I stole from my neighbor on every specimen Tonto rousted out. They don't recognize the imitations as being any different from the originals. A rabbit is a rabbit to them, regardless of those fucking little jewels."

"What about the jewels? Have you discovered what function they serve?"

"Gimme a break. I'm just starting the research and we're going a dozen different ways. Probably something to do with communication or maybe reproduction or most likely for quantum functions like levitating material back and forth while they're duplicating. Crap, I don't know yet. They won't duplicate anything while they're being watched. And any time a biologist can't tell what an organ is for he says it's for sex. Maybe that's what they're for."

"You serious?"

"Nah, I just tell the freshmen that to twist their panties. Actually, I think those three little jewels are the imitator perceptive system. They serve as sight, hearing, and ... well, something else. They must be able to scan anything close right down to the atomic level, then use those same little goddamned jewels to manipulate their surroundings and rearrange the construction of it into whatever they please -- so long as they've scanned it." Gordo mused for a moment, with his brain cells practically jumping up and down in excitement. "You know, we ought to set up some recorders. Do you realize no one has actually seen them duplicate anything? Maybe the spares are just popping up here, teleported from somewhere else. Nah. That's stupid. I need more whiskey."

"Gordo ... do you think maybe we ought to contact the military? Or the National Science Foundation or something?"

"Fuck those NSF pussies. First thing they'd do is form a committee, then a year later, decide we're being invaded. By which time every one of them would have been replaced by their duplicates with those three little jewels sitting on their bellies. Or worse, be duplicated *without* the jewels."

Damon was so startled he spit out some of his doctored coffee, much to Gordo's disgust.

"You're wasting good whiskey."

Damon reached for the bottle. "More where that came from. And I think I need it."

"Why? Not that a body has to have a reason to drink Irish whiskey."

"You just implied those things can imitate humans."

Gordo's mouth dropped open. He tugged at his beard then grabbed for the bottle himself. He tilted it to his mouth and swallowed, *gulp gulp gulp*. "Fucking damn me for an old man. So they can. It's no big stretch from a rabbit to a human. Or that fox that I think is running the show."

"But would they act like humans? Could they fool us?"

"Sure, at first, anyway. The imitation rabbits and possums are maybe a little slower and dumber than the originals but that could just be orientation problems. Regardless, they act like the originals because they all act the same. Once the process is complete no one can tell which is which. I don't imagine they'd do all that well in the wild but they're surviving here. And imitation humans could survive. Oh shit, can't you just see where this is leading?"

"All too well," Damon said, envisioning teenaged boys with an imitation blonde. Business executives with compliant secretaries. Housewives with an imitation husband in the closet. Imitation soldiers with live ammunition. He reached for the bottle again, then decided to cap it. "Gordo, we better put this up and get to work."

"Yeah. Where'd I leave my phone?"

Damon left him to search while he got on the phone himself.

***

The Testers had come to the conclusion that the brown, short-legged creature that made shrill noises was the only earthly creature they knew of (and the only one they knew of anywhere) which could identify them on sight no matter what their disguise. A wildcat that curled up for a nap after consuming a rabbit provided a possible method of ridding them of the abominable little noise-maker. The wildcat was quickly duplicated before it could wake up, then the duplicate headed toward the brick house where the intelligent species lived. It found a place to conceal itself and waited. The next morning, when the noise-maker came out to begin its activities, the imitation wildcat rushed toward it.

7

"I'm damn glad I started carrying my gun again," Damon said, touching the body of the dead imitator disguised as a wildcat with the toe of his boot. The identifying jewels on its belly were still blinking.

"This is too much," Beth said. "From now on, Tonto doesn't go out without both of us being right there, and I'm damn well going to start carrying my gun, too!" She cuddled the trembling dachshund to her breasts, shivering at how close it had been, and thanking the heavens for all the times Damon had worn his pistol in the past and practiced with it.

"Guess it wouldn't hurt for me to start going armed too," Gordo said. "Looks like the fuckers are onto us."

***

Three days later the hundred-acre farm was beginning to resemble a trailer camp run by FEMA. Two more single-wide trailers had been moved in and backhoes and cherry pickers were busy building septic systems and setting power poles.

Damon held Tonto in his arms while they both looked up the road at all the activity. Damon had relegated the new trailers to the front forty where leftover Christmas trees had been growing, cleverly getting the land cleared for free. He and Gordo insisted on the utmost precautions, surrounding the trailers with electric fences immediately upon them settling into place.

Gordo came outside and joined him and Tonto.

"Morning, Gordo. Something has to be done."

"Betcherass. The university is threatening to cut off my funding. They don't believe in aliens."

"Tonto wouldn't help them right now. He's scared to go outside and he gets nervous when he can't go to work. He trusts me to kill varmints like that wildcat, but I think he knows I can't shoot a trailer dead. And speaking of funding, who's paying us the rent for

60

parking on our property? And for all the septic systems, power and salaries for the workers and so forth. Beth instructed me to ask before she went shopping."

"Stupid."

"Who, Beth?"

"No, the dog," Gordo said. "But on the other hand, if he doesn't get out and start work, how's he going to spot the imitators for us?"

"We could build another fence and make everyone stay out of this area except the ones we want."

"Good idea. You paying for it?"

"I can't even pay for all the extra electricity you guys are using."

"Lemme get some more whiskey for the coffee. We'll think of something." The more alcohol he poured into it, the better Gordo's brain seemed to work.

While Damon and Gordo were sitting in lawn chairs outside, drinking Irish coffee and thinking, an oversized van drove up. It sprouted aerials from its roof like they had been planted there and then fertilized. A big, burly dark-haired man with a cigar stuck in his mouth got out and strode toward them.

Gordo stood up and rubbed his eyes, then grinned wide enough for it to be seen through his tangled beard. "Marco! You goddamned renegade eyetalian! What the fuck're you doing here?"

Marco Whitman never broke stride until he was standing in front of them. He removed his cigar with one hand and stuck the other out. "Gordo, good to see you. You forget to shave this morning?"

"Goddamned right, and the last 364 mornings too. Goddamn co-eds think it's cute, can you believe that shit? Damon, this is Marco Whitman. He's from the Pentagon. When they said they were sending us someone, I didn't know it would be their best meteorologist and computer expert."

"Nice to meet you, Marco. This dog sitting in my lap is Tonto. He owns the place. Did you bring money?"

Whitman blinked. "I can get some. Why?"

"Somebody has to start paying for all this crap. I can't and Gordo says the university is watching his funding too close."

"If you've got what Gordo says you have, yeah, I can get you all the money you want. But I don't believe it yet. I still think it's a plot by General Blunder Ass to get me out of Washington."

Tonto began wiggling in Damon's arms. Damon sat him down and Tonto immediately ran out to the driveway and peed on all four tires of the van while the three men watched. Then he began barking furiously, using his attention-getting alien intruder bark.

Gordo grinned. "Come on, Marco. One look and you'll be thinking aliens, too."

***

"How much money do you need?" Marco asked, once they were inside and he had examined the alien raccoon Tonto had sensed encroaching on his territory.

"Oh hell, give me a million to start with," Damon said, hoping for a few thousand. "I need to hire guards, get some fencing up, buy the land across the road, shop for supplies for Gordo, get some…"

Marco held up an oversized hand. "What you need first is a manager. I'll get you one. Next, I need your bank routing number. A million you said?"

"Uh, yeah."

"Okay, we'll call that million rent for you and I'll add enough to take care of all the other stuff." He took out a little computer and unfolded the keyboard while Damon hurried to bring some more whiskey, beer and coffee to make sure he wasn't dreaming.

***

Marco Whitman's Pentagon orders gave him almost unlimited funding and authority to use it due to the blonde PFC's lack of aptitude for clerical work. Never one to let a government mistake go unrewarded, he spent money as freely as a drunken sailor on payday after a six-month cruise. He hired a manager to get the research organized, and a lobbyist to keep the funds rolling in and the Pentagon generals placated. He combined the conglomeration of scientists, computer whizzes, physicists and nanotechnicians that he hired under one roof and named it *Project Tonto,* then slapped a top secret classification on it for the time being.

He fully intended to let the public know that aliens had invaded Earth, but the manner in which they were going about it and how it was being fought made for a difficult public relations problem. A weenie dog single-handedly (or single-pawedly) fighting off an invasion of Earth, with it being the only known earthly inhabitant that could even recognize the invaders? Marco could visualize the hash the nightly news and the talk shows would make of poor Tonto's efforts, and one shot of Gordo, with white hair trailing down past his shoulders to go with his unruly white beard and his constant cursing and drinking as he went about stymieing the aliens would get them laughed off the air, if not the whole planet.

Beth cut off courtesies of the house and its immediate environs from anyone except Gordo and Marco and their specific guests. "I like to cook," she said, "but I draw the line at cooking for an army. Besides, you guys are drinking more than eating."

"It's good for your health," Gordo said, pouring beer into the palm of his hand and letting Tonto lap it up.

The little dachshund had developed a taste for beer, as well as a liking for Damon's hairy friend. Every morning, he seemed torn between going to work and separating himself from Gordo's hair and beard and the palms full of beer. He had even begun sleeping with Gordo on the low guest bed, nestled up next to his long hair and beard, using them for a bed.

***

The Testers were increasing in number, but the fox, which was still directing operations, insomuch as it was direction rather than instinct, was becoming impatient. So far there had been no opportunity to place a large Tester such as itself in the vicinity of one of the intelligent beings long enough to duplicate it. And the smaller ones were incapable of holding a gestalt of a being of such disproportionate size in their minds long enough for a duplication to succeed.

Now, though, a whirlwind of new activity in the surrounding environment promised more opportunities. Sooner or later it was bound to succeed. If not, perhaps some of them could hitch a clandestine ride on the mechanical conveyances the sapient beings used for transport. Then they could start over in a place not so well guarded as this one, and even better, perhaps without that long-bodied, droopy-eared little demon that invariably sniffed them out and alerted its masters when any of them came near. Distance probably wouldn't be a barrier, so long as it wasn't more than a fifth of the circumference of the planet. More than that and signals tended to become garbled, even moving in a quantum environment.

***

One of the new trailers contained a veterinarian and a complete animal laboratory, along with a dozen lady dachshunds of the miniature variety, all sporting the color dachshund breeders called red but which was really a dark auburn brown.

Tonto hated to ride in a vehicle. He was certain all the noises, particularly those made by Damon's old farm truck, were uttered by monsters hiding under the seat and just waiting for a chance to eat a little miniature dachshund. As soon as Damon opened the door of the pickup while holding Tonto in his arms, he began shivering. Beth got in on the other side and took the dog.

"Poor Tonto. All this activity is a little much for a hard working little doggie, isn't it?"

Tonto whimpered agreement. He didn't like the new noises, the new people and especially the new things in his yard which masqueraded as other things. They gave off little waves of peculiar energy that irritated his brain cells, what few that were functional. He did like Damon's new friend, the one with all the nice fur and the hand always filled with that new drink that smelled good and tasted even better.

Tonto thought they were headed to town for a visit to the vet and was surprised when the truck stopped only a couple of minutes after it had gotten started. As soon as Beth opened the passenger door of the pickup, the base of Tonto's ears began jerking as he tried to make them stand up, the better to hear what he thought he was hearing. Instinct told him the noises sounded like lady dachshunds. When the trailer door opened the noises became louder, but he no longer heard them. The heavenly odor of a dozen female dachshunds in heat overwhelmed him, especially since he had never met another dog except the two wimps Gordo had stolen then returned, much less another dachshund, much less a lady dachshund in a receptive mood. He quivered harder than ever, but he was no longer shaking because of the monsters under the seat -- it was pure eagerness to get started on the business at hand. He even forgot about his job and all the work he was missing.

***

Four hours later, Tonto was back home, a sappy look on his face. His ears sagged way past their normal droop and dragged the ground on each side of him as he staggered over to Gordo.

"I see a goddamned happy dog," Gordo said, holding out his hand.

Tonto lapped up the beer, wobbled over to his bed, plopped down and rolled over on his back. He promptly fell asleep, all four feet sticking up in the air. His little tongue lolled out of his mouth in a perfect display of how a day should end for a male miniature dachshund, even if it was only a little after noon.

Damon made a stiff drink for himself and another for Beth.

"Gordo," he said, "if I had had a camcorder going, I wouldn't need any more money from the government. I don't believe anyone has ever filmed a dachshund with ADHD and only one testicle trying to service a dozen lady dachshunds in heat."

"The poor little guy did his best," Beth said. "If those girls aren't pregnant, it isn't his fault."

"He sure did. Gordo, how long before we know if it worked?"

"What do you mean? Oh. He only has one ball, doesn't he? I sure as hell hope he isn't sterile because we're going to need others like him pretty damned quick."

"Are you finding more imitators than you expected?"

"How the fuck do I know what to expect from three-eyed aliens? But yeah, they're imitating around here just a little faster than we can kill or capture them, what with Tonto being the only one who can identify them at first sight. And actually, we don't know what's going on back in the woods, do we?"

Beth gulped half her drink down, causing Damon to raise his brows. Ordinarily, she wasn't much for alcohol.

"What is it, sweetheart?" he asked.

"I don't like this. Gordo, you're supposed to be a genius. Haven't you found out what they are yet?"

"I told you. Three-eyed aliens from outer space. Dumb goddamned aliens, but aliens just the same."

"You keep saying three-eyed. Are those jewel things really eyes?"

"No, it's just a convenient description. They generate some kind of wave we've never seen before. Say, I wonder if there'd be a market for jewelry made from them? Maybe we could get hunters and gatherers into the act."

"I don't want any more people around here," Beth complained. "I have to run a godda -- I have to run a gauntlet to go to the grocery store already. And all that traffic on our little farm to market road is making potholes."

A knock sounded at the door. Marco barged in before anyone could get there to open it. He was trailed by Junie Mae and Ruthie June. He sprawled out on the big couch. One of the co-eds took a seat beside him and the other sat down by Gordo.

"Hey, Marco. How about a drink?" Gordo said.

"You're frying your brain with that stuff. Yeah, I want a drink. You know what that idiot general in Washington did? He sent a major down here to make sure this place was secure and that the media didn't get onto the fact we've been invaded."

"I'm listening," Gordo said, filling two glasses liberally with Jack Daniels and adding a smidgen of ice.

"You better. He took a live specimen back to the Pentagon with him. Now they've got imitation rabbits in the goddamn place. Then the general took a specimen over to show some senators and congressmen. Some of them keep pet dogs and cats in their offices. Now they've got rabbits and extra dogs and cats that look just like their pets and they won't let anyone touch them. And in both places, the little shits are hiding out as best they can. We're going to have to go public to have even a hope of stopping the invasion before they start imitating the congress critters."

"How do they tell the real ones from the imitators?" Gordo asked slyly, handing Marco his drink and sitting back down.

"What -- oh! Goddamn right! They're fuc ... politicians are like rabbits to begin with. Scared of their own fuc ... their own shadows." Marco glanced over at Beth.

"Go ahead and fucking say it," Beth said. "With Gordo around, it looks and sounds like we're in a third rate beer joint anyway." She grinned at Gordo to show him she really didn't mind. She liked Damon's friend simply because he was such a brilliant renegade, despite trying to hog all the beer and whiskey in Texas.

"Yeah. Well, anyhow, that's what we've got. Now I have a question? Why only rabbits and dogs and cats so far at the Pentagon and congress? I thought they could imitate anything."

"They can," Gordo explained, "but from our recordings and other data, I think they have to work up to imitating larger specimens and there weren't that many around either the Pentagon or congress. Also, we know that the bigger the animal, the longer they have to hold still before the aliens can duplicate them. Our leaders are dumber than doorknobs, but they don't generally sleep on duty; they're more likely to be screwing when they have any privacy. That kind of limits them -- for the time being. However, we need to have someone in authority put out a general directive that no large animals get into either place in the future. And in the meantime, you better get the exterminators in there quick."

"They already have. They'll get most of them, but you know they won't get 'em all. Not that it matters with congress. We'd probably be better off with the imitations than the real thing. Dumb as they are, they're still smarter than any politician I ever met. Anyway, Washington is now our hot spot. Hey, what's wrong with Tonto? He looks like he's dead."

"He's resting," Beth said. "He had a hard morning."

Gordo guffawed, spitting whiskey across the room.

8

Inadvertently, a Tester in disguise was taken on a trip and managed to penetrate one of the seats of power of the dominant species of the planet. It quickly began more duplications so that losing one of its members wouldn't be a catastrophe, and also communicated its success to the whole Tester community. The news stirred the homing instinct to greater heights and every effort in the new environment was devoted to attempts to duplicate the intelligent species, the ones that had the capability to build spaceships.

***

Over the next couple of weeks, while Gordo continued his investigation into the imitators, Marco finished getting the place organized, then turned it over to the manager he'd hired and went onto other matters. He had copies of the recordings of the two odd weather phenomena observed earlier in the year sent to the farm. He had been thinking about them ever since being assigned to Project Tonto and talking to Gordo, who thought it went beyond coincidence for Tonto to have probably been conceived during two unpredicted and completely unfathomable weather patterns. He studied the copies for a while then sent them from his trailer over to Damon's computer and followed them with his own presence.

It was almost dinnertime anyway, and Beth had invited him to take his meals in the house with her, Damon and Gordo, with the specific caveat to leave the freshmen behind. The two big-busted blondes had begun following him and Gordo around so persistently she suspected one or both of them of sleeping with Marco. She also suspected Gordo of doing the same when he went to the big trailer where they lived, always telling them he needed to do some quick "research."

Gordo had just arrived from his lab bringing news, which he related almost immediately. "Hey folks. Good news, bad news."

"Give us the good news first," Damon suggested.

"You got it. The animal lab just called. All the lady doggies are knocked up. Tonto ain't shooting blanks."

"He'll love that," Beth said. "Sporting with those girl dogs is the only thing I've seen yet that he likes better than shoveling straw. When can he go again?"

"That's the bad news. For Tonto, anyway. The lab also told me the clones we started of him are a go. Now we can be goddamned certain we'll get little pups just like him, all we want!"

Tonto, hearing his name, woke up and galloped toward Gordo. He rolled onto his back for a belly rub, then got up and eagerly lapped beer from Gordo's hand.

"I guess that tells us Tonto doesn't understand English," Gordo said. "If someone had just told me my pecker had been replaced by a clone I'd have a good case of the red ass."

Marco went out onto the porch to dispose of his cigar stub in preparation for dinner. "How much longer, Beth?"

"Half hour, Marco. You have time for a drink."

"Good. I need one. Gordo, I've got bad news, too. In doubles."

"Bring me a refill before you tell us. Tonto drank all mine."

Marco poured himself a shot of Jack Daniels neat and retrieved a beer from the refrigerator for Gordo. He came back over, looking glum.

"It can't be that bad, Marco. Come on, spit it out," Gordo said.

"Okay. First, the imitators are duplicating themselves, and not only producing more rabbits, but they've started on the mice and rats in the Pentagon and both houses of congress. And we still haven't convinced the stupid congress critters and their staff to leave their pets at home, so by now we may have aliens all over Washington. We'll never clear them out now, not without complete evacuation and sterilization. And this morning there was a scene. A secretary in the Senate office building went to sleep during her lunch hour and when she woke up, she found her twin self sitting at her desk doing her nails. At first she didn't recognize herself but when she did, she screamed bloody murder. So did the other one. Now no one can tell which is which, other than one of them keeps talking about space travel and the other about clothes and boyfriends."

"Crap and shinola," Damon blurted out. "Gordo, I thought you said they had to work up to duplicating large animals."

"I'm sure they do," Gordo said. "And I thought we had quarantined that building for pets so one place would stay relatively safe. Marco, do you know whether or not anyone in the building sneaked in a pet ... no, wait! Don't the guards use German shepherds for security and bomb sniffing?"

"Ah, shit. You're right. Why didn't we think about that?"

"They were gonna get loose sooner or later, so don't feel too bad. You said that was the first bad news. What the fuck is second?"

"The aliens aren't very smart, but it appears they have a survival instinct. One of my bright boys told me yesterday he thought some of them were learning to conceal their little jewels, even after being seen with them at first. He sent a specimen along and Tonto identified it today. Alien, big as Sicily, but no jewels. They were gone."

"What about the secretaries?" Beth asked from the entrance to the kitchen where she was standing, watching the stove and listening in on the conversation at the same time.

"I don't know yet. They both refused to bare their bellies last I heard."

"How stupid. They go out in public with everything from their nipples to their crotch showing but won't pull up a blouse?"

"Yeah, I know. The congressional doctor has been called in. I sent word what to look for but he hasn't called me back yet."

Gordo consumed a shot of Jameson's to go with his beer and his mind went into hyperdrive. "You said some of them are learning to conceal their jewels. From what I've learned of their genetic makeup, I'm pretty certain they have two sexes at least, and probably three, except we haven't seen the third one. I'll bet just one of the sexes can conceal their jewels, or we'd never have seen any to begin with. Damn it to goddamned hell, that's going to complicate matters even more."

Damon looked over at Tonto, who was lying on his big pillow and gazing at Gordo with love in his eyes. Or perhaps watching alertly on the chance Gordo thought to pour some beer into his hand for him. "How soon will Tonto's pups be ready to go to work for us?"

"The ones Tonto had fun producing are over a month from birth. The clones will be a week or so behind them. Old Mossback has got us a building by the local airport. Every day, miniature dachshund females are going to be flown in, impregnated, and flown back to four or five special kennels for care. Soon as the pups are ready, they can go to work."

Damon and Beth exchanged glances. Damon let Beth tell them the bad news.

"You guys have obviously never had many dogs around you. Don't you know a pup has to bond with humans before it will develop

70

naturally? The new pups won't perform worth a flip if you don't have good homes lined up for them."

Gordo's flummoxed look was priceless. Without thinking much about it, he poured his palm full of beer and reached down to let Tonto, who had watched the operation avidly, gallop as fast as his short little legs would carry him over to the beer.

"Well, shit," Gordo said, wiping his hand on his beard. "I never thought of that. I guess right after supper, I better rouse old Mossback out and tell him to get busy and find homes for them. That's gonna fuck up trying to keep this whole thing secret, though, even without what's happening in Congress. Give a bunch of broads a mama dog with pups and they can't resist telling every female in Texas about them, not to mention the other states." He mused for a moment. "Probably best to go ahead and get it on out and see what the crazies will do when they know it's a real invasion and not something thought up in a wet dream."

"Who the hell is this Mossback you keep talking about?" Beth asked, ignoring his reference to women as broads. It was just the way he talked and no one was ever going to change him. Beth thought she wouldn't even want to. She got too many laughs out of him the way he was, an atavism who should probably have been born a caveman.

"Mossback is Hans Mausbacher, the general manager of Project Tonto. Who the hell did you think it was with a name like Mossback?"

Beth rolled her eyes, then laughed when Gordo winked at her. "Oh, well, of course I should have known. Okay, before we eat, or get too drunk to think, you said you had some good news, Gordo. What was it?"

"Oh. I can't be real certain yet, but from the looks of what passes for telomeres of the critters I've studied, they won't live all that long. Anywhere from a few months to few decades, depending on the species of animal."

"What's good about that when they can duplicate more of themselves? Or whatever they're posing as."

"They've got a peculiar gene structure. I'm still working on it but it looks like their sex chromosomes are missing a piece or two. Like I said before, I think they have three sexes, which means they need a third sex in order to propagate naturally, so to speak. And so far neither me nor Marco's bright boys have seen but two. One with jewels, one without -- or with them, but hiding them in another dimension."

"You mean the invasion might be self-limiting?"

"Damned if I know. Too early to tell. That third sex that's missing, if it is, might be here, but be rare enough that we haven't spotted it in any of the little fuckers we've dissected so far."

**

Mausbacher called a general meeting several days after shrapnel from all the bombshells Tonto and the imitators had caused cooled off enough to handle. He also had more news. He gave it while they were all sitting around the kitchen table with coffee and beer.

"We have our first duplicate congressperson, Sheila Johnson Leemay. She's going bonkers, not but what I didn't think she was bonkers to start with."

"Wait," Damon said. "Which one?"

"Which one is bonkers?"

"Yeah."

"Both. One is screaming for the president to do something and the other is screaming for the army to take over rocket research and build a spaceship and when they're not doing that, they're screaming at each other and both trying to sit at the same desk and both claiming they're Sheila Johnson Leemay."

"Jesus Christ and Kitty Mess, too," Beth complained. "One of them has already made Houston the laughing stock of the country, what with sticking her nose in front of any camera within fifty miles of her, and now we have two of them?"

"Yep, but forget about her. We've got real trouble. We've got twin senators from Massachusetts."

"Oh, goddamn!" Gordo cursed. "It's too early in the morning for this crap." He looked around the table. "Damon, you're not saying much."

"I was wondering why one of the Sheilas was agitating for a spaceship; that's all. And wasn't one of the duplicate secretaries talking up space?"

"So is one of the senators," Mossbaucher said. He didn't see the significance of Damon's remark. He kept his report straight, causing Gordo to start thinking of something else. So did Damon. Eventually their eyes met across the table and they nodded minutely to each other.

As soon as their manager had finished updating them, Damon went over to his wife. "Sweetheart, Gordo and I need to go do a little research. We'll be gone for a while."

Beth eyed them with female calculation, decided they were innocent for the moment, and nodded. "Okay, but take some beer with you so you won't interrupt me while I'm making some cookies."

"Yummie," Damon said, giving her a big smooch.

He and Gordo began walking and drinking their beer. Tonto spotted them. He looked at the piles of straw he had already created that day and decided he could take some time off. He trotted over to them and began following. Every few minutes he ran a little ways ahead, stopped and peered up at the beer cooler in Gordo's arms. If he couldn't see that clearly, he could smell what was in the can Gordo was carrying.

"Will it work?" Damon asked, assuming Gordo would know what he was talking about.

Gordo knelt down and let Tonto lap some beer before answering. "It might. Two cases don't make a universe but if the pattern holds, it might. Of course, we could very well get shot for even thinking what we're thinking of doing." His phone rang. Gordo cussed but answered it. He listened for a moment then hung up. "One of my contacts says the president is getting all uptight about duplicate congress critters." He snorted. "As if a few more would make a bit of fucking difference, what with all things they fuck up. And get this. He doesn't believe there's an alien invasion at all. He thinks it's some kind of political trick to ruin his re-election chances."

"How about congress? Did your contact say anything about the trends there?"

"About the same. The dumb shits are each accusing the other party of using clones from secret labs to foul up reputations."

"How many years will a human duplicate live? Did you say decades?"

"Yup. If my research holds, and I think it will."

Damon nodded. "If the duplicates keep wanting to speed up space development, that's one way of telling them apart."

"Yeah, but a lot of ordinary people believe in the invasion, and they want to see space travel get going so we can go whip the asses off the BEM's."

"So, what we have to do is convince the world that Tonto or his pups or his clones really can smell them out, huh?"

"Right on, except for our purposes, it might be better if Tonto is the only one who can do it." Gordo squatted down and petted Tonto with a few strokes of his hand then stood back up. He pointed to the dog. "He's the key, of course. You keep saying he's a bit addled. That's okay, but can you train him to do what we're thinking of?"

73

Damon's normally bland face drooped a little. "Neither Beth nor I have had much luck. The only thing we've ever been able to teach him is to fetch one squeaky toy. Just the one and no other. Besides that, he just doesn't listen. He's fixated on his sticks and straw and the garden hose. And beer since he met you."

"Well, he's the key. Hmm." He looked down at the little dachshund that was sitting on his haunches and looking back up at him. "Tonto, little fellow, how well do you like beer?"

Damon's face brightened as if suddenly lit with a ray of sunshine. "By God, as much as you've gotten him to liking it, that might work!"

"Okay, why don't we try it?"

"You mean…"

"Goddamned right. We'll be ready in case the clones or pups aren't alien-sniffers. By the way, I've now got four co-eds working for me. Apparently, they took a nap too close to that big hound dog I used to experiment with that the captive possum duplicated. And guess what? They both think spaceships are as neat as Marco's mustache or my beard."

"Do they have the jewels?"

"How would I know? Gordo stared at the sky, trying to look innocent.

"Don't bullshit your friends. Yes or no?"

"No. I checked each one of them out while I kept the other three locked up. It damned near killed me."

"How so?"

"They wouldn't let me stop with just pulling up their blouses. I had to screw them, too."

"I feel your pain, Gordo. If you're not too tired why don't we get started and see if Tonto will go along with the gag?"

"Suits me. But it's your turn if they want to get screwed again."

***

"What are you and Gordo up to now?" Beth asked a few days later. "Every morning, you and him and Tonto go trotting off to that trailer where the co-eds live and spend two hours there."

"We're just doing research, sweetheart. I promise."

Beth pursed her mouth in a half smile. "I don't think I completely believe you. Why don't you invite them to dinner tomorrow?"

74

Damon couldn't think fast enough to get out of it. "Um ... uh ... well, okay. But you can't ask them about the research. It's secret. If it gets out, it'll spoil everything."

"Well, make sure it doesn't rub off on you, big boy. Just because we've got the only alien-sniffing dog in the world and the government is paying us a million a month rent for our front pasture, don't forget who makes your cookies and fluffs your pillow at night. Understand?" She winked at him.

"Gotcha. Just no questions for right now, okay?"

"Okay," Beth agreed reluctantly. "For now." She didn't press because she was already suspecting what her husband and Gordo were up to and wasn't sure she wanted anything to do with it. On the other hand, she had always supported Damon in his endeavors, no matter how goofy, such as the idea that he could make a living writing, or growing Christmas trees. If it hadn't been for her salary over the years they'd have been in the poorhouse long since.

***

The next day at dinner, Beth opened the door for her company. Damon came in first, followed by Gordo, with Tonto trailing behind him. Marco was next. After that, the two freshmen co-eds followed and Beth started to shut the door to keep the flies out. "Whoops, sorry!" She blinked. "I must be losing it. I thought you two just came in." She held the door open and the two young women came into the house. Beth shut the door and turned around. Now she thought she was seeing double.

"Wait a minute! What's going on around here?"

"Research," Gordo said.

"Research," Damon said.

"I don't know," Marco said.

Woof! Tonto said.

The four young women said nothing. They just smiled as two of them seated themselves on each side of Gordo and the other two on each side of Marco.

"I don't believe any of you," Beth said. "I know when men are up to funny business and you two are in it up to your necks." She pointed a finger at the freshmen co-eds. "And you young ladies are in it up to your ... your..." her voice trailed off as she suddenly realized she must be speaking to aliens!

The two men did their best to look innocent but were only partly successful. The only reason Beth didn't get the frying pan after

Damon was because she sensed he was telling the truth. He just wasn't telling all of it. They were up to some tricks with the co-eds, alien or not or which or what. She decided to let it be, but found it very hard to be polite to the "young ladies."

During the meal, Gordo said as casually as possible, "Hey, I heard the government might be getting interested in a crash program for a new spaceship. Have any of you heard anything about it?"

"That's great," two of the freshmen said, but no one knew whether it was Junie May, Ruthie June or the imitations.

"We watch the news," another one said, implying that they were the only ones in the household interested in world affairs, but not mentioning that Gordo had ordered them to so he wouldn't have to be bothered.

The dinner went downhill from there, since neither Damon nor Gordo would talk about their research and Gordo had given strict orders to the co-eds not to, on pain of canceling their part in the study. The warning was not only as effective as duct-taping their mouths, but it pissed Marco off since he wasn't being included in it.

"You're going to have a part to play, Marco, just be a little goddamned patient will you?" Gordo said.

Marco gave him the evil eye, inherited from one of his Gypsy ancestors. "I'd better have, or your fucking funding is gonna be looking awful goddamned sad."

"No problem, Marco. Shucks, Beth is gonna get in on it, too."

"I am? That's news to me," Beth said.

"I lobbied for you, babe," Damon said, giving her a wink across the table.

***

The Testers knew the humans, as they had found they were called, were up to something with the females, both alien and human, but they couldn't quite figure it out. The Tester duplicates, even in the guise of humans, weren't quite as intelligent as the beings they were imitating.

***

That night in bed, Damon spilled the beans when Beth asked him again about the research in her most compelling, alluring fashion. Put that way, he was unable to resist, as Beth had known. After she was finished with him, he gave up the secret, or most of it anyway. He omitted the part about how the freshmen insisted on breathing heavy before showing whether or not they had the jewels.

After hearing the plan, Beth woke up Tonto with her near-hysterical laughter. Tonto was sleeping with them for a change since Gordo was working late. So he said. But after the laughter died, she hugged Damon very tight. What he was planning really wasn't all that funny. "Sweetheart, are you really sure you want to do this?"

"Name me a single congress critter who doesn't deserve it."

Beth remained silent, then sighed. Her husband was right, much as she disliked the concept.

9

The Tester community was happy. They had succeeded in duplicating a number of the reigning sapient species, some of them in positions of power, and in the area of the planet where the power was exercised. Their quantum methods of communication enabled most of them to know what was happening. The most astounding thing to the leaders was the lack of real resistance to their plans for getting back home. There was some quarreling and disputes about methods, but no violence. And amazingly, many of the ones responsible for directing human affairs didn't even believe they originated off-planet. The Testers had never heard of such a state of affairs, much less been involved with such an odd sapient species.

The only thing hampering their plans, so far as they could see, was being able to duplicate enough of the humans. Whether or not they believed in aliens, they saw the beginning of a groundswell of resistance to duplicates of themselves running around, even if the others couldn't tell the difference. Nevertheless, they began to believe it was entirely possible to return home while they were still sexually viable and able to combine with their third sex, thus enriching their masters with data on a wonderful world, one they would surely want to return to, and bring them back as well.

***

"They're slowing down on imitating humans," Hans Mossbaucher said one morning a few weeks later when giving his weekly management update. Beth had invited him to the breakfast table for events. "Or I should say the precautions our leaders are finally beginning to put in place are beginning to slow the number of duplicates, at least among those who believe in the aliens instead of political dirty cloning tricks.

"Good," Gordo said. The research was going very slow because Tonto wanted his beer without working for it.

"But the president wants to declare martial law."

"So why hasn't he?" Damon asked. "Does he still not believe us?"

"Because most of the people who know about it still think it's a big joke of some kind. Your place here is still on the secret list and only a few people know about Tonto. Which reminds me, the head of the Senate Intelligence Committee wants to sequester Tonto as a "national asset.""

"Over my dead body," Beth said. "Besides, it wouldn't do any good. He won't listen to anyone but us, and he doesn't even listen to us that much."

"I know. That's what I told him. It quieted him down some for now. Next, the first batch of Tonto's pups has been whelped. They all look just like him, so in only six more weeks they'll be ready to go to work."

"But what if they don't turn out like Tonto? They only have half his genes, you know," Beth said.

"We've still got the clones. They're about ready to debut, and they'll be his exact twins."

"Good. I hope they work because I don't want poor Tonto to have to spend all his life going around identifying aliens. He already has one job. I still have my doubts, though. Just because they're clones of Tonto doesn't mean they're the same."

Mossbaucher didn't get it. "What do you mean, Beth? Of course they're the same. They're *clones!*"

"You tell him, Gordo," Beth said.

Gordo tilted a can of Coors to his lips, drained it, and tossed the can over his shoulder, scoring a perfect two points in the trash bag, as usual. "Moss, ol' buddy, while they are genetic twins of Tonto, they weren't raised like him. Environment influences expression of genes. Besides, they weren't conceived when or where Tonto was, which I believe has lots to do with his abilities, and I ain't talking about shoveling fucking straw, either."

"Oh," Mossbaucher replied in a very subdued tone of voice.

"What else do you have today?" Damon asked. He was anxious to get back to the research.

"That's all for now."

"Good. Then Gordo, Marco and I have a request."

"Speak up."

"We need you to convince a few of those duplicated congress critters to come out here on an 'inspection trip'. And we want them to be males. And we want both the original and the duplicate."

79

Mossbacher screwed up his face, causing his eyebrows to twitch. "Why males?"

Damon explained. "We need to be sure of some research we're doing. We know it's applicable to female duplicates and their originals, but not males. See?"

"No, but I'll connive some reason to make a few of them want to come see you."

"Wonderful."

Outside, a few minutes later, Marco accompanied Gordo and Damon toward the research trailer. "Junie Mae and Ruthie June spilled the beans. I think I know what you guys are up to."

"Uh oh," Damon said.

"Crap," Gordo said.

"What's wrong, guys? I approve. There's just one thing I want understood."

Raised eyebrows greeted his statement and invited him to continue.

"First, we need to get a move on. General Blunder Ass has gotten suspicious about all the money I'm spending. If we can't find a way to calm him down, our funding's liable to be axed."

"We'll think of something," Gordo promised. "What else?"

"If those male twin congress people that're coming out here want to be screwed before they show their bellies, you can find someone else to do the job."

***

"That damned general in the Pentagon has suddenly decided to come along on the inspection trip," Marco announced disgustedly that night at dinner.

"You think that's bad?" Beth said. "I heard on the news today that Sheila Johnson Leemay made a place for herself on the inspection team too, then of course her twin says she's coming. One of them was bad enough, but two of those broads in congress is liable to set democracy back a hundred years."

"Damn it all to hell, and we need to do our research while they're here," Damon said.

A devilish grin suddenly appeared on Gordo's face. "Folks, you just leave it all to me and I think we'll come out of this shindig in good shape."

Woof! Tonto agreed.

80

When the conglomeration of congress people, the general and all their aides and hangers-on and reporters showed up at the gate the next day, Damon was cordial and pleasant and immediately began offering drinks all around. Marco was affable and friendly and insisted on keeping everyone's glasses filled to the brim. Beth was suspicious and wary and kept Tonto close at hand until Gordo showed up and insisted they needed him for "research purposes." A handful of beer and Tonto was agreeable to almost anything.

Gordo, citing secrecy and the delicate nature of the research, refused to allow anyone into his research trailer except General Blunderous, the two Sheila Johnson Leemays and two sets of twin male congressmen. By this time they were all a little wobbly.

Several hours later, the group departed the research trailer. The males were tousled and guilty looking. The Sheilas were disheveled and even more guilty looking. General Blunderous was drunk, happy and didn't look a bit guilty.

Six freshmen co-ed duplicates of Junie Mae and Ruthie June waved happily from the door of the trailer. The extras had been allowed to duplicate in order to service the "Inspection Committee."

"Bye bye, General," a Junie Mae said.

Bye, Sheila, honey," a Ruthie June said.

"Bye bye, you sweet little General, you," a Junie Mae and a Ruthie June said in tandem.

"Bye bye," the other Junie Maes and Ruthie Junes waved to the male congressmen.

As soon as they were out of sight, and everyone was gathered back at the house, Gordo rubbed his hands together and laughed. "So much for that problem. I never saw a congress critter yet that could resist a little poontang. And I've got it all recorded."

"How about Sheila Johnson Leemay?" Beth asked.

"I slipped both of them a Mickey, but I really don't think it was necessary. It turns out our Sheila Johnson Leemays go for freshperson co-eds, too."

Beth laughed and shook her head. "Gordo, you'll never be able to talk politically correct, so please don't start trying now. It just makes you sound silly."

***

Gordo's trap settled the funding problem for the time being and for the first time since being elected, Shelia Johnson Leemay began avoiding cameras rather than chasing them. And around the capital, the number of duplicate congress people continued their slow increase. They talked about space travel. Bills began to be introduced into the house and Senate that would greatly increase funding for space research. Strangely, the wording dictated research of a particular kind that no one had ever heard of.

10

At six weeks old, Tonto's pups from the first batch of lady dachshunds he had been introduced to were brought from their pen to the house and put down on the tarmac of the driveway. Marco turned off the electricity in the cage he was holding and dumped out a dozen baby rabbits, half of them real and half alien, then everyone stood back.

Tonto looked to Damon for instructions before he did anything, showing that his training was coming along. Seeing no sign from him, he went almost crazy trying to identify the fake rabbits while they were hopping and scattering all over the place.

His pups were interested but gave no indication whatever that they could tell the difference between fake rabbits and the real thing. Even after Tonto went around to all the ones he could still find and identified the aliens by barking, the pups could care less which were which, which was natural since they obviously didn't know the difference. They simply wanted to chew on them all.

Gordo reached down and picked up one of the rabbits Tonto said was fake. He turned it over. "No jewels," he said, and put it in his pocket. He picked up another one. "This one has jewels. One of the sexes is still disguising their jewels somehow. Maybe by shoving them off into another dimension. And they're obviously communicating back and forth with those in Washington, because the ones around here didn't start disguising themselves until the ones there did." He put the rabbit with the three little jewels on its belly in another pocket.

"How the hell can they communicate that far?" Marco asked. "And why are you stuffing them in your pocket? Marco was smart but a far cry from Gordo's intellect.

"They send signals either with a special wave length the jewels use or through quantum effects. I think that's it but be goddamned if I can prove it, being the goddamned observer and all that shit. I hate quantum fucking physics. And I'm putting these two in my pocket to dissect. The last two dissections showed one sex has the jewels showing and the other doesn't. If it holds for three in a row I'll call it a wrap and quit fucking with them."

"That's not the immediate problem, Gordo. Things are getting hairy in Washington, what with more and more congress persons and senators having duplicates that we can't tell from the real ones."

"Well, crap, Marco, just tell them to shoot the ones that talk about spaceships if they're in that much of a goddamned hurry. That's a sure way to ID them if they won't undress and let someone look at their bellies. Of course that's not a sure thing, either. But what the hell, no one'll miss them if the wrong ones get shot. What's one politician, more or less? Washington is overrun with the fuckers and you ask me, they all need shooting."

"We can't just go around shooting congress critters out of hand, much as they deserve it. It would cause talk," Damon admonished.

"Well, Tonto is not leaving here for more than a day at a time," Beth said. "He'd miss his sticks and his straw. And if he goes, I go with him. Although, here lately he seems more interested in that research of yours than his straw or the garden hose." Then she remembered. "That's okay, though. Whatever makes him happy."

"I'll get Mossbaucher to tell the president to wait for the fucking clones to mature," Gordo said. "But if they come up a bust, we're gonna have to go to goddamn sonofabitching Washington." He grinned in spite of himself. "I almost hope they do fail. Can't you just see every one of the congress idjits that have a double all being made to file past me and Tonto, you and Damon and Marco while we give 'em either a thumbs up or thumbs down, just like the old goddamned emperors in Rome did for the gladiators."

Damon pictured the scene in his mind and began laughing so hard he spilled half his beer on the tarmac. Then he quit laughing. The situation really was becoming very serious. Demonstrations pro and con were a growing phenomena and space travel was on everyone's lips, either for it or against it. Half the population believed America was being invaded by aliens and the other half thought the first half had lost their collective marbles. He knew something was going to have to give soon. In one way he hoped desperately that the clones would be like Tonto and able to identify the alien duplicates, and in another way he hoped they turned out to be normal little miniature dachshunds, interested in food, belly rubs and playing fetch like normal dogs, even though that would put him and Gordo in great danger. Him, especially.

84

Tonto was off the mark and after Damon's spilled beer and began lapping happily. He was joined by a gaggle of fat little dachshund pups trying to get a lick in too.

"Like father, like son," Damon said happily.

"He's not your son, you idiot, he's a dog," Beth corrected.

"I was talking about the pups."

"Same difference. You're still not a dog."

"You're not making any sense."

"No one has made any sense around here since those bug-eyed monsters showed up," Beth declared.

No one could argue with that.

***

"The story's out and the pro-invasion faction is in charge," Gordo said. He and Damon had taken a rare day off from their research and were half drunk from sitting around in the cool of the house drinking beer all day.

Damon watched the news unfold on the television set in the den. The cameras in congress panned in on several congressmen and women who stood next to their exact twin, other than for clothing. Both Sheila Johnson Leemays even had their hair done in the same style, no mean feat even for a BEM. All the twins stared daggers at each other, unlike the freshmen co-eds living in the trailer. Those seemed to get along fine, so long as they were visited each day, which was one reason Damon and Gordon were taking a day off. They were both totally exhausted and had explained to the co-eds that neither of them were supermen and they wanted to relax and watch the news for a change.

As they watched, every single one of the congressional twins spoke up loudly, each claiming to be the authentic person. With them all talking at once it was a babble and hardly understandable.

"*As you can see,*" the anchor said, "*we have plainly been invaded by monsters from outer space which can duplicate our very own leaders. So far, scientists have been unable to devise a method of determining which is the real person and which is the fake.*" The scene faded out and another took its place, showing giant cranes hovering over the congressional buildings and swinging wrecking balls. "*President Gush has ordered the congressional buildings to be torn down. Soldiers are standing by, ready to shoot any living animals which come out of the ruins. For the ones too small to shoot, other soldiers are holding nets, ready to capture the aliens for later disposal.*"

85

The camera panned in to show a soldier holding a butterfly net, not a very good portrayal of how the nation was being protected from invaders. Apparently realizing it, the camera hastily swung back to the female reporter on the scene, a very pretty blonde.

"How come all the reporters these days are good looking blondes?" Beth asked.

"Who cares?" Gordo said. "They may have pretty faces but their tits suck."

The blond reporter tried her best to look very serious as she spoke. *"The president's press secretary has indicated that President Gush has been aware of the problem all along but avoided mentioning it for fear of panic. Rolendi?"*

"Thanks, Kimberly." The anchor picked up a random slip of paper on her desk and pretended as if it had just been given to her. *"Yes, President Gush has been aware all along of the severity of being invaded by aliens who can imitate any living creature, right from the beginning, Josh Jacobs, the presidential press secretary says, but the president wants it to be known that he and his staff have been working day and night trying to find a solution which will repel the invasion. He is proud to say that the ongoing research has come up with an answer, which will be announced shortly, thus ending the problem."*

"Those stupid asses!" Gordo shouted at the television set. "We haven't even tested the fucking clones yet! We don't know whether they'll be able to tell the difference or not!"

"But shouldn't they, if they're a clone of Tonto?" Beth asked. "I know about environment and all, but the ones I've seen sure look like him."

"Theoretically, yes, but the proof's in the fucking pudding. You got any scissors around here?"

Beth blinked at the abrupt change of subject. "Women always have scissors somewhere."

"Good. My beard is so long it's catching on my beer can when I take a drink. I need to whack a few inches of it off. Besides, we may be on TV soon and I want to look good."

Beth exploded with laughter picturing Gordo's long white hair hanging around his shoulders, trailing down his back and front both, and in front merging with his voluminous, equally white beard, but she went to get the scissors while the national news anchor continued to blather and call on one pundit after another for their expert thoughts on the subject of aliens on Earth. The program went on and on but nothing else of any significance was ever said.

Gordo carefully trimmed off three inches of hair and two inches of beard, or at least he thought that was what he did. With them so intermingled, it was hard to tell.

86

The nation was scared, mesmerized, appalled, angry, irate, horrified, aghast, terrified and shocked. They demanded that something, anything, be done and be done immediately and weren't prepared to take no for an answer.

The United Nations assembly voted a quarantine of the United States. The United States ambassador vetoed the resolution. The Security Council took up the debate. The president said he had instructed their U.N. ambassador to veto any resolution isolating the United States and threatened war against any nation which cut relations with the country. It did no good. No one wanted to go to a nation where they might find themselves suddenly in the presence of a bug-eyed monster which looked just like them.

Reporters, snoops, spies, undercover agents, terrorists, stringers, cults, busybodies, Internet surfers, hackers and world savers of every color, kind and stripe scurried here and there and schemed everywhere trying to find out the secret the president said would be used to repel the invasion. Inevitably, someone found out. A thirteen-year-old computer hacker discovered that somewhere in the United States lived a miniature dachshund that could tell with one hundred per cent accuracy whether someone or some animal was real or an alien in disguise. A ground swell of impatience demanded that the dog be impounded and brought to the capitol and put to work weeding out imposter congressmen and women and senators.

"It's time to bring out the clones and hope like hell they work," Gordo said at dinner a few days afterward. "Otherwise some young Archimedes is gonna find out where Tonto lives and the whole goddamned United States Army won't be able to keep busybodies away from us. In fact, we'd better ask for protection right now."

"Are the clones old enough?" Marco asked.

"Seven weeks. If they can't do it now, they'll never be able to. Let's go test them."

"I'll get in touch with Washington and get some soldiers out here to guard the place. Our security force wouldn't stand a chance against a mob of pro and con dachshund groupies."

"Go. Don't waste a second. Come on, Damon. Let's try our clones."

***

The clones performed no better than Tonto's puppies had. They sniffed, woofed and scampered around sniffing and chasing rabbits but not one of them could tell the difference between a real one and a fake.

Just on the chance that there was something special about the rabbits, Gordo and Damon also tried the clones on opossums and mice and even the freshmen, but got no better results.

Gordo sighed and squatted down with Tonto. He held out a handful of beer. "Tonto, little fellow, it looks like you've got the world on your shoulders. Get your traveling paws on. We're going to Washington."

11

It wasn't all that simple. The National Science Foundation, the FDA, Homeland Security, The Dachshund Breeder's Association and a plethora of scientific, pseudoscientific, and other concerned and interested bodies insisted on Tonto proving his mettle on a nationally televised hookup broadcast to the whole world, but first they insisted that he show his acumen in private.

Tonto did so, performing perfectly under the sharp eyes of the judges, working long hours with mice, rats, rabbits, other pet dogs that had been twinned and several unimportant clerks and secretaries until the observers were completely satisfied. Tonto was declared competent to sniff out aliens by the most prestigious Blue Ribbon Panel ever assembled in Washington.

Gordo wanted to make an announcement first, telling of his research which showed that the aliens presently on Earth would eventually die out anyway because they lacked the crucial third sex necessary for normal propagation and that the alien critters needed to be studied in order to discover how they manipulated quantum phenomena. Furthermore, he wanted to tell the world that the aliens were essentially harmless and would be of inestimable value in developing interstellar space flight so that humans could venture out into space, hunt down the miscreant aliens and punish them, if not obliterate them completely.

When Damon, Gordo, Marco and the rest of their group arrived, the president took one look at Gordo's appearance with his long ragged hair and beard and shuddered. Not him! Even Marco gave him qualms what with his cigar, a political incorrectness if ever there was one. The president was a politician, after all, and worried about such minor displays even when connected with an alien invasion. Anyway, the president said, it didn't matter a whit whether the aliens would die out or not; the people wanted action now! Gordo gave up in disgust and took his co-eds into a guest bedroom at their hotel with a fifth of Jameson's and a case of Coors. He locked the door and wasn't seen until the next day.

Damon suggested another committee of Nobel Laureates do the judging of Tonto's veracity and it was accepted by President Gush, the house and Senate leaders. Unfortunately, it took some time to gather them and even more time to decide which ones would be on the committee. The Nobel prize winners were human beings, after all, and fought tooth and nail to be selected for the honor of helping to save the Earth from bug-eyed monsters.

Even when Damon thought it was all settled, Saudi Arabia led the organization of petroleum exporting states in a declaration that an embargo would be placed on oil shipments to the western world if some Arabs weren't on the committee.

Gordo came out of the bedroom where he had been hibernating for days with the co-eds and saw the news bite. "Fuck them goddamned ragheaded motherfuckers!" he shouted. "Goddamned stupid fuckers aren't smart enough to figure out their religion stifles original thought so they substitute oil for imagination. Tell 'em to go fuck a camel."

"I'd love to, Gordo, but we've got to get going on this thing. Look at that mob out there! They're gonna overrun Washington if the politicians don't get this settled pretty damn quick!"

Gordo blinked his bleary eyes at the big screen television. It showed hundreds of thousands of protesters, all united for a change, and all demanding the same thing: Get the aliens out of our city! Get the aliens out of our country! Turn Tonto loose!"

"Hot diggety damn! I love it! Now's our chance to really clean house and get the space program rolling besides. Has anybody figured out why so many of the twins are agitating for a crash program for building spaceships?"

"Of course not. Hell, all that mob out there wants the same thing. They want the government to hurry up and build spaceships and go bomb the aliens."

"Shit. We don't even know where they're from."

"It doesn't matter much. If those aliens really know how to build a spaceship, we'll find them. They'll tell us themselves, most likely, if they're in such a hurry to get home to their third sex," Damon said.

"Right on. Well, I guess I'm ready if you are, whenever..."

The phone rang.

Damon picked it up. "Damon Stone here." He listened while his face showed a growing horror. He put down the phone and turned to the rest of the group.

90

"What is it, sweetheart?" Beth asked.

"The aliens have gotten into the White House. Our stupid president brought his pet Labrador to the oval office and a hidden alien promptly duplicated it, and then it was big enough to duplicate the president while he took his noonday nap in that little room behind the Oval Office. Then it got worse. Now we have two chiefs of staff, two press secretaries, two chairman of the joint chiefs, two homeland security secretaries … and two presidents!"

***

President Gush was declared unable to discharge his duties and the vice president took over the reins of government. The vice president wasn't a real politician and had only allowed himself to be put on the ticket as a favor to a friend who had invested a fortune in the president's political party. The situation changed rapidly with him in charge. He declared martial law. He set the army to rounding up every single congressman, senator and any other official who had been duplicated -- both of them. He also insisted on the president and his twin being rounded up, too. He put them all in confinement at the nearest sports stadium, surrounded it with an army division, and called Damon, Gordo, Marco and Beth to bring Tonto to the arena and get busy and no nonsense allowed.

"C'mon, Tonto, you're on," Damon said.

"I'll bring the beer," Gordo said.

"Make sure you bring enough for you and Tonto both," Beth advised.

"I wonder what they'll do with the aliens after Tonto identifies them?" Marco said.

"They oughta put 'em in front of a fucking firing squad," Gordo said, winking at Damon.

"Yeah, that's what they oughta do," Damon agreed.

***

Damon's face blanched white after their party was led through the bowels of the stadium and out onto the playing field. Most of the seats along both sides of the fifty-yard line were filled with observers from around the world. At one end of the field, posts had been set up. Thirty yards in front of the posts waited a firing squad.

"Oh, my God!" Beth said as she took in the scene.

"Oh shit, Gordo, do you see what they're gonna do?"

"Goddamned right I do. Don't weaken now."

Damon gulped and nodded. He had been about half way kidding all along with his and Gordo's plans, but now they had been hoisted on their on petard.

Beth closed her eyes for a moment then set her mouth in a tight, unsmiling line. She remembered her conversation with her husband when he asked her to name one politician who didn't deserve what was about to happen. She looked at him and nodded grimly, letting him know she was behind him, all the way.

*****

The twins were made to stand in a long line, side by side and the show began.

Tonto whimpered and looked up at Damon.

Gordo filled his hand with beer.

Damon gave Tonto the signal. The little one-balled, ADHD affected, cross-eyed miniature dachshund went to work. At each supposed alien he barked, loudly and long. He passed half of them by without making a sound. As each of the ones he barked at was led to a post, Gordo fed Tonto some beer from his hand.

Tonto paid not a bit of attention to the screams of protest and denials when he barked at an alien. He was doing his job and wouldn't be swayed by anything, except a pause now and then to lap some beer from Gordo's hand.

Before they even got to the end of the long line, the firing squad went to work. After Damon and Gordo were finished, Damon put his arm around Beth and whispered, "Ignore it, sweetheart. Those sorry bastards deserve it and everybody in the country with a lick of sense knows it." Then he had a dire time trying to ignore the sounds of the rifles firing in unison himself.

*****

The ordeal was finally over with. The president was reinstated in office. Congress was cleared of aliens. The world was happy and unified. Everyone took Gordo's and Marco's word for it that the twinned animals would die out fairly quickly.

Damon assured the public that Tonto would be available whenever there was a question of whether or not a human was an alien in disguise.

Beth insisted that such tests must take place on the farm, that the suspect men and women must come to Tonto from now on, not the other way around.

Tonto went back to work shoveling pine straw and soon forgot about beer after Gordo went back to the university, to vast acclaim. The two remaining freshmen went with him. They flunked their freshman year for missing too many classes and were forced to repeat. They didn't seem too unhappy about it.

And late one night Damon and Beth talked.

"Were the firing squads really necessary?" Beth asked her husband. "I thought I'd faint when I saw what they were up to."

"You weren't the only one, sweetheart. Me, too. But you know in your heart, every single one of those men and women were guilty of putting their own ambitions before those of the country, and almost all of them were outright crooks. And now look. We've got a real space program even if most of the congress persons who were so insistent on it are going to be dying off."

"It's no wonder. Gordo said they would." Beth chuckled despite herself. "And just to prove how dumb politicians are, not a single one caught on to yours and Gordo's scam."

Damon laughed, too. "Yeah. You know, we really didn't intend to go through with it at first. We even hoped the clones would work so we wouldn't be tempted. But once push came to shove, we decided we'd been right all along. We did the job. And by golly, Tonto performed like a champ. Once I gave him the signal, he skipped every one of the aliens and barked at the politicians."

Now Beth laughed out loud. "It's mean of me, but I can't help laughing at the expression on their faces while they were denying they were aliens."

Damon laughed out loud, too. "Which proves no one ever believes anything a politician says to begin with!"

THE END

TONTO:

AN AUTOBIOGRAPHY OF AN ODD, ADDLED, AUTISTIC DACHSHUND, AS TOLD TO HIS MASTER

Foreword

This isn't really a science fiction story, but what other category do you put the story of a talking dog in? Especially when it's the story of the dog who was the avatar for the science fiction novel *Bark!* And finally, a talking dog makes it science fiction in my book, even if he did do it only that one magical night.

When you read about what Tonto has to say for himself, you may have trouble believing a dog would think that way, but it's all true, I swear. I listened to his tale as he lay in front of the fireplace with me on a cold winter's evening. I don't know what happened that made it possible that one time for me to understand dog language, but I took advantage when it occurred and wrote it all down. I sat still and let Tonto talk. That's when I discovered I didn't know my dog near as well as I thought I did but, after all, I was the one who asked him to tell about his life in his own words and in his own way so you would know what a really…um…exceptional dog he is. You see, Tonto is sort of addled and…but this is his story. Let him do the talking. You just kick back and read about his life and enjoy yourself. That's what I did, even though I knew a lot of it already.

That one cold evening by the fire when Tonto suddenly began talking gave me an entirely different perspective on a dog's life. Maybe it took a full-time author plus a special dog and a special evening to make the magic of understanding dog language work. It's never happened again, which is perhaps just as well. Tonto is pretty much full of himself already, to hear him tell it. If it got to where he could talk and make himself understood any time he wanted, no telling what kind of additional trouble he might get into—and he gets in enough as is. Just read what he had to say that one time and you'll understand.

Darrell Bain.

BEGINNING

Hello, humans. My name is Tonto. I'm a dachshund dog, which in case you don't know is the finest kind of dog to be, especially if you get in as much trouble as I do. Long wiggly type dogs can escape predicaments better than those big brutes like German Shepherds and Labradors. Besides, I'm a special dog. You see, I have Doggie Asperber's Syndrome. That's a kind of autism that makes people sort of addled but also allows them to concentrate their efforts when they have a mind to. That's how come my master can understand every word I say right now, because I'm focusing so hard. Sometimes Master calls me strange and thinks I have ADHD and well…yes, I guess I am a little addled, but it's not my fault. I was born this way. I'm also cross-eyed and can't jump and have trouble chewing and have no sense of direction which is why I used to get lost so often, and I was born with only one testicle but that's no real handicap. I functioned better with one than most dogs can with two when I still had it. Just ask that lady dachshund across the road, and if she could talk she'll tell you that's the absolute truth.

I'm always getting into trouble because of my handicaps but I can't help it. Did I tell you how the thunder monsters are always after me and the vacuum cleaner monster and the airplane boogers and the car monsters and lots more. If you had all those boogers and monsters always after you, I bet you'd be a little addled and prone to trouble too, wouldn't you? I guess it's a good thing I have a lot of lives like those dern cats do because I sure have used up a lot of them. Being so unusual like I am and having all those handicaps don't bother me a bit because I have a good master and mistress and they take good care of me even when they do get aggravated at me. They know monsters and boogers are out there and don't like me so they're sympathetic.

Once you've heard my story, you'll also understand how I became the avatar for my master's science fiction novel *Bark!* where a little weenie dog like me not only saves the earth from a strange type of alien invaders but helps you humans get rid of a bunch of crooked

Washington politicians while he's at it! Only a dachshund doggie like me could have managed that feat. By the way, that story has been published in digital form too, and so *Bark!* is available now as an e-book at www.fictionwise.com and www.ereader.com My master was very happy about this book being in print too and gave me lots of treats for serving as the model for the doggie in that story, but shucks, I would have done it for nothing. Heck I can't help it. I'm just the way I am and he wrote a story about a dog like me. I haven't seen any aliens yet, but I bet I could take care of them just as good as that dog in the story did any old day. The Tonto in *Bark!* is fictional but this story of my life is true. I am my master's miniature dachshund, Tonto, the only tool-making and tool-using dog anyone has ever heard of or read about, and also the oddest little dachshund anyone has ever seen. I am truly one of a kind, and I am a perfect example of the phrase; "Marching to the beat of his own drummer." That's how I got to serve as an example for that story, *Bark!*

I have not exaggerated a single episode here. I am a good example of the old adage; "Truth is Stranger Than Fiction". I honestly don't know how I have survived as long as I have, but as my master and mistress say, I hope he goes on for years and years, amusing and amazing them as I go my happy bumbling way through life, completely unaware that I am different than other members of my species. They think I honestly believe I am a real dog! Shucks, I know I'm real. I'm telling you this story about my life, aren't I? They're not going to argue with me, that's for sure. I'm money in the bank as soon as this is published. Who knows? One day aliens may actually arrive on earth. If so, be at ease. Tonto will protect you!

ME AND SUSIE

Every time my humans look at their two miniature dachshunds, with their short little legs and floppy ears, Master laughs when he thinks of how we are descended from wolves. But heck, if we could manage the mechanics of it, we could actually breed with a wolf. What self-respecting little dachshund would want to, though? They believe it's funny to think about our ancestry, even knowing we would never be able to survive in the wild, especially me who is afraid of just about every creature on earth except butterflies. I'll attack a butterfly in a New York Second if it threatens either my master or mistress with harm, but that's about as much as a cross-eyed, autistic dog who can't jump or chew very good can do.

After they lost their other beloved dachshund, Biscuit, which they thought was the smartest, most lovable and most people-oriented dog they have ever been owned by at a tragically young age (his life story is available in both e-book and print editions under the title *Doggie Biscuit!*), they eventually got far enough past their heartbreak to think of obtaining another dog. Of course they never expected to replace Biscuit. He will live forever in their hearts and those of many other people who have read his biography, *Doggie Biscuit!,* but life does go on. After Biscuit, their first dachshund, nothing else would do but another dachshund. I mean really, after being owned by a dachshund, would you want to be bossed around by any other dog? Don't be silly!

First they took in a female black and brown short hair that they named Susie. She is a nice enough doggie, except for being mean and kind of dumb, but at the time she didn't seem to be very people oriented. Her main goal in life appeared to be that of barking at anything and everything all hours of the day and night, perhaps thinking she was protecting her new owners and her new territory. For some reason they got the idea she might be lonely for companionship with her own kind since she had been accustomed to having other dogs around at her former home. The reason the owner gave for selling her was that she was too small to breed, but I suspect now that the woman just couldn't stand the constant shrill yelping. The noise doesn't bother my people too much though since we all live on a big place out in the country in East Texas and she has lots of room to roam. She can go outside any time she wishes and bark her fool head off. Still, they thought she would be happier with another doggie around and they thought perhaps that might quiet her down. One day they saw an ad in the local small town newsletter about dachshund puppies for sale. After talking it over they decided to go look at them and that's when they found me.

I COME TO LIVE WITH MY MASTER AND MISTRESS, DARRELL AND BETTY BAIN.

My mistress told the lady selling us pups they wanted a male if she had one. She left, then returned holding three squirming, grinning little dachshund puppies. One of them was only about half the size of the others. That was me, of course. I was born small, along with my other oddities.

"Are these from the same litter?" Mistress asked.

"Yes, the small one is just the runt." I objected to that, but at the time I didn't know how to make my master understand me. I probably still couldn't except he is an author and they can do funny things other humans can't.

Mistress was already holding me when she asked the question. I had a slightly different appearance than the other two pups, which were the classical "red" dachshunds. I was darker. Some of the fur along my back and shoulders is almost black. I was really a distinctive little guy, if I do say so myself, despite my small size.

Master and Mistress exchanged glances. Both of them had immediately become sympathetic, thinking of the struggle such a little guy must have had amongst his larger littermates. And they could tell I clearly wanted go home with them. They looked like nice humans to me and if I didn't take them, no telling what I might get. I was already struggling with all my might to get to Mistress' face and give her some doggie kisses.

"Here, hold him while I get the checkbook," she said, making up her mind. I give great doggie kisses. In case you ever visit, and I allow you to get close, check me out.

I went right to Master, of course, and we bonded immediately, especially after I gave him a few face licks and he tickled my floppy little ears. They had no idea at the time there was anything wrong with me other than my diminutive size and I couldn't tell them, of course. It would soon become apparent, though. I couldn't conceal my oddities but by then it was too late. I owned them.

MY PROBLEMS EATING AND DRINKING

Perhaps I was born with a trouble gene along with all my other oddities. Shucks, I got into a fix even before my first visit to the vet for my next series of shots. Even before that, though, they noticed something funny about me.

I do not and will not eat like a regular dog does, gulping down his food in a hurry, especially when in the presence of another doggie like Susie, who doesn't mind trying to eat her food and mine, too. I'm much more refined than most dogs. I take my time eating and savor it instead of gulping in down in two or three big bites. They have to guard my food, first while I decide whether it's something I even want to eat to begin with. If it's anything at all new, outside of my regular diet of lean bologna and cheese and diet dry food, I may or may not eat it, but in any case it's going to take a while. I don't like to make decisions about important things such as food in a hurry. Maybe other dogs do, but not me. I'm much more refined than that. I circle my food bowl to make sure something hostile, like a mean old bug or like that isn't lurking in it. Finally I'll approach the bowl and peck my nose at the food, like a chicken eating, but still not taking a bite. I don't smell too good and it takes me a while to decide. I walk away and come back several times with the same routine while I'm making up my mind and Susie is already finished and going half crazy because master and mistress won't let her come eat my food, too. It became very exasperating to them until they finally realized I wasn't just being contrary—there was something wrong with me. Since I can't smell as well as a regular dog I have to really check new food out. For all I know it might be poison. And when I do eat, it is very slowly, as if I'm having problems chewing and/or swallowing, which in fact, I am. Every time I take a drink from the automatic water bowl, I gag after I'm finished drinking as if I'm going to barf—but I never do. It's just the way water goes down after drinking from a water bowl that makes me do it. I'd much rather drink from the garden hose, but for some reason the humans won't bring it in the house for me.

Treats? I will hardly eat treats, no matter what kind. If it's put down by Master when Susie isn't around I may occasionally try one, but only after sniffing, pushing it around with my nose, backing off and looking at it from several angles and probably walking off then returning several times. You have to be sure about food, and like I said, I'm more refined than other dogs. I've got manners while eating, not like Susie and some other dogs I could name.

I will not accept food from anyone's hand. They may be trying to poison me. It has to go on the floor so I can inspect it first, going through my usual peck and sniff and peck and circling it until I'm sure it's safe. A dog who can't smell as well as other dogs has to take more precautions, don't you know?

I have finally gotten to the stage where I will take a miniature vanilla wafer or bits of cheese or little bitty pieces of peanut butter cookies from Master or Mistress' hand, but only after going through my usual routine with the first bite. After all, someone could have come in and changed the cookies in that box while I was outside and put bad ones in the place of the good ones. A doggie can't be too careful these days. Of course my people have never even heard of a dog eating like this, much less seen it before and they've had lots of doggies. They've just never had a special one like me before, that's all, and it took me a while to train them in my eating habits. They're pretty fast learners, though, so I guess I'm lucky I got them and not some dufuses.

Actually, my diet is pretty simple, too. I'm so finicky and suspicious about food that I forced my humans to experiment a lot to find out what I would and wouldn't eat. With Susie, it doesn't matter. She is a glutton and will eat anything, so they figured whatever I settled on would probably satisfy her, too, and naturally, that's the way it worked out. Susie isn't all that bright, sad to say, but the poor girl can't help it.

The two basic food groups for me wound up being bologna and cheese. I gets one slice of bologna a day (lean turkey bologna now since I've started growing those damned love handles, but it really doesn't matter whether it's lean turkey or fat beef bologna. If it's bologna, I'm satisfied). To that is added half a slice of American cheese. I usually eat after just a minute or so if that's all that's in my bowl, but sometimes Mistress adds table scraps for variety. It doesn't fool, me, though. I'm wary about anything new. Mistress will put meat trimmings or a bit of leftover hamburger in the bottom of the bowl and cover it with my cheese and bologna, but she can't fool a smart dog like me, even if I am autistic and probably have a touch of ADHD besides. I may not be able to smell as well as a regular dog but I can smell some.

If anything extra is in my bowl it takes me longer before he I'll begin to eat, and even then I'll eat only the cheese and bologna, leaving the scraps. Then comes the sniff and peck routine for several minutes to be sure it's not going to hurt me. I'll usually accept most scraps but I'm not about to get in a hurry over them. Even when Susie began gulping hers first and stealing my food, it made no difference. Anything new in my bowl is automatically grounds for suspicion. I've heard of dogs being lulled into eating all kinds of bad medicine like that. They finally had to begin feeding me and Susie separately in order to make sure I got my supper, but I don't mind putting them to a little extra effort. After all, they're here for my benefit, not the other way around.

With dry food, I eventually got used to it, and its presence in the big food bowl which Susie and I share doesn't bother me since it's always the same stuff. I am different there, too, though. I eat dry food from the bowl by laying down first, then wriggling forward until my head is over the bowl. It looks as if I'm the laziest dog on earth when I'm doing that, but I'm anything but lazy. That's just one of my ways of conserving energy for other things. In fact, I stay so busy that I'm over three years old now and I have never yet had to have my nails trimmed. It's a good thing, too. Derned if I would sit still for that buzzing little monster gadget that eats on Susie's nails after they're trimmed by Dr. Bob. Susie is a couch potato and has to have her nails done every month, so if you ask me, that buzz booger is no more than she deserves.

Now back to the trouble. I did say I can't seem to stay out of trouble, didn't I?

MY FIRST TIME LOST

It's probably a good thing that my people were both retired when I decided to go live with them, because it turned out that I required more attention than they thought they had bargained for. On the other hand, they got to be owned by a very special dog, so they should consider themselves lucky. Mistress had been retired for several years from nursing while Master had back trouble and some other medical problems that finally induced him to close their Choose 'N Cut Christmas tree farm a few years earlier than he had intended to and become a writer. It's too bad, in a way. I would have made a great Christmas tree farm doggie with my special abilities. On the other hand, Master turned to writing full time and so he got to tell the whole world about me, which is a good thing. That's even better than Christmas tree farms if you ask me. There's lots of those farms and only one of me. They did still live on the farm when I came along, along with two of their grown human pups and their families who built on the land my humans gave them. Both Master and Mistress worked in medicine a good portion of their lives and they both truly admire the way they saw parents of handicapped human puppies endure the extra care and attention those pups need. It is the same for a handicapped little doggie. It takes a lot more time and effort to care for me than for a regular old dog, but they get their money's worth. I bet no other human is owned by a slightly addled, ADHD afflicted, autistic, cross-eyed doggie who can't jump, has problems eating, has no sense of direction and gets into all kinds of death-defying predicaments. They are so lucky.

I had been with them for only about two weeks. I was about two months old, perhaps a couple of weeks older than that but not by much. They had begun letting me out on my own when Susie went out, hoping that she would help teach me that the house was not my own personal bathroom. I went out one afternoon with Susie about two o'clock. Susie came back a couple of hours later, but I had disappeared. What happened is that I got bored with her barking at every silly thing in the world and decided to strike out on my own for a while. I got sort of turned around and the first thing I knew I had lost sight of where I lived and Susie was jealous of all the attention I was getting so she stopped barking and went home, leaving me to find my own way. I must have gone the wrong way because the next thing I knew it was getting dark and I naturally couldn't sniff my own trail back home because of my faulty nose and besides, I ran into three giant mongrels that scared the bejesus out of me.

My people missed me and hunted up and down our road for me, calling my name and recruiting that worthless Susie to help. All she did was lead them deliberately on a lot of false trails to be sure they didn't find me. She's a heartless dern female, I think, leaving a little puppy out like that. By six o'clock I was still gone and they extended their search for me. They went into the woods, and up and down the county road about a quarter mile from our house. No Tonto, of course, because I was hiding from those monster mongrels and by then it was dark and there were other boogers and monsters around the area making weird noises that sounded like they would just love a little puppy for supper so I kept quiet and stayed hidden. It was getting late and naturally they were becoming very worried since I am so special and they didn't want to lose me. They hunted on our private road again, the county road again, then they went to the neighbors on each side of us and asked them to keep an eye out for a little dachshund pup. Our nearest neighbor's house is several hundred yards away. They are the ones I learned later that belonged to those three really large dogs, nice friendly mutts they had rescued after people dropped them off on the county road, but I was still new to the territory and I couldn't tell they were friendly. Besides, they were so dern big and clumsy if any one of them had stumbled and fell on me I would probably have been crushed to death. I don't know why anyone would think every person living in the country would automatically want to have a large dog running around their place, especially since most humans in the country already have dogs of their own already, but people wanting to get shut of dogs they don't get along with will just take them out and leave them. They are cruel and should be neutered, if you ask me, to teach them some manners and make them be nice. Anyway, Master doubted I would go over to that house, not with those three big dogs living there, but he told them about me anyway, which shows what a good master he is, so concerned and all about me. There are three related families living in three homes on that property. They all said they'd watch for me, even though it was already dark. I heard all this of course, but I couldn't come out of my hiding place because of the monsters and boogers, and remember I'm cross-eyed and couldn't see very good in the day time much less at night so I figured I'd better just stay where I was for he time being despite how worried I knew my people would be.

By nightfall, I still hadn't shown up, of course. My humans continued searching until almost midnight, using flashlights, sometimes walking, sometimes driving the car or truck. Finally, they accepted what they thought was the inevitable. They thought I must have wandered off somewhere and either got stuck in a hole I was exploring or gotten lost in the woods and couldn't find my way home. That last thought was actually pretty close to the truth except it was Susie who took me out and got me lost then left me. Females are strange, aren't they? Can't get along with them, can't get along without them, but where would we be without them? Anyway, they both naturally felt horrible but they had done everything they could. I stayed where I was but I couldn't sleep because of so many monsters and boogers out at night making noises and I didn't know which were good and which weren't so I didn't trust any of them.

The next morning, Master went outside well before daylight, hoping I had come home during the night, but it was only a hope. I was nowhere around, naturally. During the morning my people searched some more, calling and calling, imagining all kinds of horrible contretemps I might have gotten into. Master even went to the local animal shelter and left a description, just in case someone did find me and turned me in, but he had really lost hope by then. Both of them felt miserable about losing such a special little pup like me, but there was simply nothing else they could do. They searched some more during the morning, rather forlornly, knowing it was almost certainly useless, but they felt obligated to try.

And then…about eleven o'clock, a golf cart appeared on our road, driven by Ben, our neighbor. Cynthia was with him. And in her arms was me, their little lost dog, alive and well.

After they held me and loved me and shed some more tears over my safe return, they learned what had happened, or what Ben and Cynthia knew about it. They couldn't ever know all about what happened because I hadn't learned to talk yet and wouldn't for a long time, not until Master started writing for a living, which made me decide to talk and tell him all the things about me he didn't know. Remember, these neighbors of theirs are so soft hearted that they take in stray dogs when no one else will. Bright and early the next morning they began searching their property since Master had told them the day before I was lost. I believe it was Cynthia, or perhaps her mother, who lives in her own home there, who had the idea that I must have come over to visit and been scared by the big dogs. A pretty smart human for a female, you have to admit. She began looking around, especially by the guest cottage, where there's just enough room for a small animal to get under it, but way too close to the ground for anything like their big dogs. She said she bent down and saw the two big brown scared eyes and the head of a little doggie looking out at her from beneath the cottage. She called softly again and again and finally coaxed me out and into her arms. She told my people the poor little fellow had obviously been frightened and taken shelter under the cottage and there he had spent the evening, all night, and the next morning, hiding. She didn't say what a smart thing it was to do, but I think Master and Mistress figured it out. A little puppy not much more than two months old made a pretty smart decision, they thought, and of course I have to agree. I may be odd, but I not a dummy.

They thanked the neighbors profusely and vowed they would watch me closer from then on, for you see they still hadn't realized I had vision problems. And it must have been a more frightening experience for me than I thought it was despite my cleverness in hiding because ever since then I have had nightmares. The nightmares would get worse over time as I continued to get into trouble and had more bad things to dream about, but that's life. Some pups get the cream and some get the skimmed milk and a fellow has to take what he's born with and be satisfied is the way I look at it.

MY PROBLEMS WITH VISION

You already know about me being cross-eyed by now, but Master and Mistress were just getting the idea. They had already noticed I couldn't navigate the steps Master built for me to get on and off the porch, which is every bit of eight inches high at the closest spot to the earth, real high for a pup that sees everything double and sometimes triple—and sometimes not at all! The porch also has regular steps, but they were still a little big for me. Master put some flat two by fours on each step of the three to give me something not so high to climb up and go down. Still, I frequently missed my footing and tumbled the rest of the way down. Little pups are naturally clumsy and it sure doesn't help matters when a fellow sees two or three steps when there's really only one there, does it? I had lots of trouble climbing up, too but eventually I managed it. My problems with the steps gave them their first inkling that I might not see as well as a normal dog, but the real indicter came a little later.

Master was in his easy chair with the footrest up and had me on the seat beside him. He was sleeping the last time I glanced at him, and wouldn't wake up so the next thing I did I was walk out to the edge of the foot rest and leap off. I could see three floors and the first one looked close but it was just an illusion from my faulty vision. It was just like a dive, a perfect up and down arc. Unfortunately, it wasn't a pool I was diving into but a hardwood floor. I landed squarely on my punkin head with a thump seemingly hard enough to shake the house. Boy, did that hurt!

I yelped and cried and wailed, even after Master picked me up and held me and petted me and told me he was sorry for not watching me more closely, but that didn't make that bump on my head hurt any less and sure didn't keep it from swelling up, either. And it dern sure didn't make the floor come any closer so I never trusted it again. I finally quieted down and I licked Master's face and cuddled against his chest for a good half hour just to let him know I was okay, then I allowed him to very carefully set me down on the floor. I wasn't wobbly and didn't appear to have any permanent injuries other than a big bump

111

on my head, but it still worried Master and Mistress. I was about due for my shots anyway, so they took me in to the vet, Dr. Bob.

Just getting me into the dadgummed harness was a struggle (they bought me one I have to wear when going to the vet, like the one Susie wore when she went to the vet). I was scared of getting tangled up in the thing, especially with Master trying to put it on me because he's not very bright when it come to stuff like that. After he fumbled around and got it tangled and had to start over a couple of times, I was fed up with the whole business. Even after it was on I cowered down and wouldn't move, just to show him what I thought about the whole sorry business. Why should I have to wear a contraption like that to visit the vet? Like going there isn't bad enough to begin with, I have to be all tangled up in that silly thing, too. I hated it. In fact, I hated it so much and complained so much that Master finally shopped around and found what is called a "Hug-A-Harness" which fastens by Velcro and is simple enough for even him to operate and that solved the problem.

Riding in the car scared me almost to pieces, especially when the big eighteen wheelers passed. They made a horrible racket and I couldn't see good enough to tell what kind of monsters they were so they scared me even worse. Not knowing what kind of monster is lurking right outside the car is awful, let me tell you, especially one that roars and makes the car shake when it passes. Master might want me to sit up when we were in the car, but I insisted on lying on the floorboard between his feet rather than on the seat with him. I told you, I'm not dumb, and that was the safest place I could find. My humans know now that the blurry scenery outside scared me because I couldn't see well enough to tell what was happening, but at the time they couldn't understand why I didn't want to sit up and look out the window.

Our Vet, Dr. Bob, gave me a thorough exam. It really wasn't all that bad because he knows enough about doggies, especially little pups, to know we want to lick a stranger's face and get a taste of him so we can tell if he's an okay person or not. After he leaned his face down and I licked it good, I decided he tasted fine and let him go ahead and have his fun.

My people were very happy that he could find nothing at all wrong with my head and he took a look at my jaws or teeth to see if that might be causing my trouble with eating, but he didn't find anything out of the ordinary. Perhaps it was a result of something that happened in the kennel where I was born that caused me pain or other problems with eating, Dr. Bob said. Perhaps since I was the runt of the litter, the other pups mistreated me when I attempted to eat and made me fearful of food, but since I couldn't talk, he really had no explanation. They just had to accept it for the time being. Actually, Dr. Bob wasn't far from wrong. I was so small I always got the leftovers from the other pups in the litter and sometimes it wasn't all that great, which makes sense if the other puppies wouldn't eat it, and that's how come I'm always cautious with food and all.

My vision was something else. Dr. Bob said he thought I was cross-eyed. That was why I was having problems navigating the steps and why I had leaped from my chair, probably thinking the floor was closer than it actually was. He was dead on right about all that, but I couldn't say so, so I didn't. He saw no signs of a concussion or injury from that plunge that ended with my head hitting the floor dead on. That was a huge relief to Master. He had been feeling guilty ever since (and still does, even though it's three years in the past now), but shucks, he didn't know and I've forgiven him a long time ago. He ought to just leave it be like I have.

There was a problem Dr. Bob found that I hadn't anticipated, though, and neither had they. One of my testicles hadn't descended properly, by gum. It wasn't causing me any immediate problems since I was still so young I didn't have much use for it anyway yet, but Dr. Bob warned them that it would make me more susceptible to cancer in that area later on if they didn't have it fixed, or have me neutered. I didn't know what they were talking about at the time or I might have made a break right then and really tried to get lost but since I had no idea what it meant, I forgot about it. Since there was no immediate danger and I wasn't having any problems with the undescended testicle, my humans decided to delay that decision until later. They told Dr Bob the little guy was already afraid of enough things in his life, what with not being able to see clearly, and they were sure right about that. If you can't see what it is, you gotta be scared if you're smart enough to come in out of the rain.

I was very glad to get out of the harness, which they removed as soon as we were back in the car. I still insisted on cowering on the floorboard, though, rather than sitting in Master's lap while Mistress drove. Heck, he knew I wasn't to blame. If he was a human pup and all he could see from a car window was a blur of threatening objects that made loud noises, he'd probably cower as far away from the windows as he could get, too!

MY FIRST SNAKE BITE

Snakes are treacherous, slithery critters that wiggle around on their bellies and have sharp teeth and smell like frogs and are about as smart as a doorknob, but they can be dangerous. A few weeks later, Master thought I was old enough to leave with Susie while he and Mistress ran a few errands, especially as I hadn't shown any more tendencies to stray after that scary night under the guest cottage next door, cowering from what he probably thought I thought were monsters all around me in the darkness.

They were gone about two hours. In the meantime, that dern Susie was busy getting me in trouble again. I swear, she wanted me to get killed so she would be an only dog again. She introduced me to a snake and told me it was just something nice to bark at and why didn't I join her at it? So, since I wasn't doing much else at the time, I did, except I sniffed instead of barking (I wasn't barking yet). When our people drove up, Susie wasn't on lizard patrol at the back door where they park. She is a real lizard dog and in my opinion ought to be changed into a lizard for the way she treated me when I was small. She usually likes to show them she's on duty when they drive up after being gone for a while. I wasn't in sight, either, because Susie had gotten me in trouble with the snake. I found out it didn't like being barked at or sniffed at and could do something about it if a pup got too close. They called out. Neither Susie nor I answered but they could hear Susie's shrill yelping coming from the other side of the house, where the pump house for the well and the unused bedroom patio are. They didn't like the sound of the bark, as if she had something cornered but was afraid to attack. Neither did they like the fact that I was nowhere in sight since I was still a pup and still learning my way around with no one but a dumb female like Susie to teach me. I sure am glad human females aren't as stupid as doggie females are, or Susie is at least. I don't know too much about other female dogs but if they are all like her I feel sorry for them.

The people both hurried around the house to where the barking was coming from, and sure enough, Susie had a copperhead snake at bay, coiled up and ready to strike. I was there, too, but I didn't seem very enthusiastic about the process, which was only natural since when I got close to the snake and tried to talk to it I saw two of them with my faulty vison and one of them reached out and nipped me. It hurt like the devil and I backed away and sat down. I decided right then that snakes were mean and I didn't like them even a little bit. I liked them even less when the place where I had got nipped kept hurting worse and worse. Our humans found out why I wasn't participating in the snake baiting with Susie a few minutes later after Master ran for the hoe and killed the snake, which served it right for hurting me. With my impaired vision, I had already been bitten. They thought I had probably walked right over it and the snake got me in the lower hind leg. They didn't know how Susie told me I could fool with it all day long and nothing would happen. One of these days, she's going to get it for being so mean.

They took me in to see Dr. Bob as quickly as possible—and I believe that was the last time they ever had a dog bitten by a snake when he had his office open. Like human pups, doggie pups don't seem to get injured at convenient times.

I got a steroid shot, a shot to help with the pain, some antibiotic pills, and some more pills for pain. They dreaded the sight of all those pills because already I had made up my mind that I didn't like pills, of any shape or kind. They taste bad and I never know why they want to give them to me. My aversion to pills may have been partly Master's fault. Shortly before the snakebite, he had tried giving me my first heartworm pill by following the same procedure he had used for Biscuit at first. He held me in his lap, stuck the pill in my mouth and rubbed my throat. It tasted raunchy so I spat it out. When he tried again I began struggling and, stupidly and stubbornly, he persisted. He finally got the pill down, but it was a long year before I would sit in his lap again without becoming suspicious and struggling to get away if there was a pill anywhere within fifty feet, and I learned to sniff them out and see them even with my bad eyes and faulty nose. I hate pills.

I can't remember now exactly how Master managed with the snakebite pills, but it was poorly. I don't think he ever finished my antibiotic regime and I was able to only get one pain pill down after the shot wore off because I hate swallowing the pesky things. They don't go down right. Fortunately, I was young and healthy (other than the oddities that kept cropping up) and threw off the effects of the copperhead venom after a couple of days. It scared my people but did no lasting harm to them—a good thing, because my poor eyesight would result in more encounters with snakes. That dern Susie ought to warn me when they're copperheads, but she never does. *She's* not the one who'll get bit.

I GET LOST AGAIN

I had barely recovered from my first snakebite when that mean old Susie took me out and lost me again. When I realized she had gone off and left me in the woods, I got frightened but I decided there was nothing to do but find a good spot to hole up in for the night and try to find my way home when it was daylight and I could see a little better. My night vision is even worse than it is in daylight. Just imagine seeing two or three shadows each cast by moonlight of mangly trees and bushes waving in night breezes and I bet you'd be scared too. Master and Mistress went through the same routine as before, searching high and low for their cross-eyed little dachshund, only now they were even more concerned about me. I had made a place in their hearts already with my goofy grin and my stumbling, bumbling way of getting around, appearing to be happy so long as I wasn't thwarted in whatever I wanted to do, which was plenty. I like to stay busy, not like that lazy couch potato Susie. They didn't know it at the time, but this single-minded determination to stay busy was the first signs of ADHD or perhaps a form of canine Autism that would grow more apparent over time. And of course by now they knew I had problems with eating and drinking, but despite all that, they were glad they were the ones I had picked out to go home with because they didn't think anyone else could take care of me as well as them.

Despite searching even harder and more thoroughly than the first time I got lost, and extending the area by a half mile or so, they didn't find me. I had found an abandoned Armadillo hole and I wasn't coming out even when I heard them call, because I was sure I'd get lost trying to find them in the dark and a booger would get me for sure. They even went deep into the woods searching for me, fearing I had gotten trapped in brush or a hole, but they never came near enough to me to get me to come out of the hole. Besides, a mean old bobcat was in a tree nearby just waiting on me to crawl out and I sure didn't want to have to fight him, little as I was. Dachshunds were bred originally as badger dogs, with their purpose in life to go down badger holes after the animals. Naturally they like to explore tight spaces and narrow tunnels or holes. That's where they thought I probably was and they were right, but I wasn't coming out until daylight. They searched with flashlights until midnight, calling and calling. I felt sorry for them but I couldn't take a chance on leaving my hole with all those boogers and monsters that prowl around in the dark, not to mention that Bobcat just waiting on me to come out of my hole so he could have me for dinner.

They even enlisted Susie to help, but as before, she pretended they were playing games even when she knew they were looking for me. She wanted me to stay lost. She's just mean to me. All she did was lead them on numerous false trails and around in circles while pretending like she had no idea at all they were looking for the new member of the family. After a while they thought perhaps she didn't even want them to find me. They knew her nose was already out of joint anyway because, nice people that they were, they had taken in a stray right after they had Susie spayed, and for almost a week she was overwhelmed by the frisky stranger until they finally located the lost dog's owner. Then not too long afterward they brought me into the home, which Susie thought was *her* home. Females are like that. They think homes belong to them and no one else. At any rate, my people finally abandoned the search and collapsed into bed, having given up for the night.

The next morning, bright and early, they began hunting for me again, with the same negative results. They came back home for coffee and a rest then went back out. See what good people they are? Lots of humans treat dogs like…well, dogs, but Master and Mistress know doggies have more sense than other animals, especially cats and female dachshunds, and they were really concerned. This was just about the time their daughter and son-in-law, Pat & Rob, let Brownie, their six month old dog, out for his morning run. At the time he had yet to be neutered and roamed a good bit. Each morning he crossed our place, followed some trails in the woods around our homes, and then went over to see the neighbors and their big monster mongrels. Brownie is a mongrel too, get right down too it, but at least he's not built like an elephant. You have to admit though, that purebreds like me are the top of the doggie totem pole. Mongrels are unpredictable as you'll see later on. Anyway, this was the regular circuit Brownie made, morning and evening and he just happened to come near where I was just backing out of the armadillo hole I had hid in during the night.

"Hey, Tonto. What you doing out here this early?" he asked.

"Aw, that dern Susie took me out for a walk yesterday and left me out here. I can't smell too good and couldn't backtrack to my home."

"That's a female for you, boy. Well, just follow me, I'm heading that way now."

So that's what I did. Mongrels have their uses sometimes, I have to admit.

Brownie came back from his morning trip through the woods and from his regular visiting spots about a half hour later, and there I was, an exhausted and very bedraggled little dachshund behind him, running as fast as my tired little short-legged body would go. Master and Mistress could tell right off I had obviously been lost all night in the woods and Brownie had providentially found me and brought me home. They were ever so grateful, and loved up on Brownie almost as much as they did me, which I thought was taking things a little too far. I mean he's only a mongrel after all and I'm not only purebred, but a purebred dachshund. They took my tired little body inside, where I drank about a gallon of water, cleaned out my food bowl with no urging or nit-picking and collapsed on my bed, dead tired. Being lost all night so young is very exhausting in case you haven't ever had the experience, and having to be led home by a mongrel was embarrassing to say the least, so I wanted to lay down and take a nap and forget about the whole thing. As soon I was fast asleep, my people noticed my little body twitched and yelped and they knew I was having bad dreams about those scary old woods. They never knew where I spent the night, of course, but they knew I must have found me a little hidey hole or I would have been eaten by a big wildcat or set upon by coyotes and they are perfectly correct about that. There's monsters everywhere out in the country.

That was my last time to ever wander far. I guess that second time I learned my lesson. The big outside world is not meant for cross-eyed little dachshunds to explore, not in depth, ever again. I ventured over toward the neighbor's a couple of more times but never went farther than a certain point. I might follow Susie to the edge of the woods, but never again would I trust her enough to venture into them with her. I was content to bark at the varmints from the safety of the yard and let her run along the game trails and chase armadillos and opossums. That's after I learned to bark, which didn't come easy for me, but more on that later. Susie chased varmints but never intended to catch one, like Biscuit regularly had, you understand. She is a barker, not a fighter. And I was forever afterwards content to bark from the porch at varmints who ventured into the yard. My hearing is pretty good, even if I can't see or smell very well. I know when an intruder is around and I warn Master and Mistress but that's all I'm big enough to do.

TRAPPED

In my short life, I've been involved in so many travails, scrapes, and different kinds of trouble that they all tend to run together in my memories. It's not that I'm continually in trouble; it's just that I've gotten into jams so often that, in looking back, it seems like it was just one painful, annoying or scary thing after another. I guess that's what I get for being special and I sure am glad I figured out early how those silly lazy cats manage to have so many lives, because it turned out I really needed the information or…well, I don't like to think of the alternative. Do you?

Soon after my scary night lost in the woods, I got lost again. I know, I said that was the last time and so it was in a way. This time I wasn't lost, though. I knew exactly where I was. Master and Mistress didn't, though, and thought I had wandered off again. This was a really bad experience, but for a curious and determined little fellow like me, it's probably inevitable that I keep getting in fixes like the one I'm getting ready to tell you about.

I was still very young and hadn't yet explored all the nooks and crannies and tight spaces dachshunds like to find out about, that is unless you're a couch potato dachshund like that lazy Susie. If she had done her job properly, she would have already found out about this place and warned me, but she didn't of course, not only because she is so lazy but because she still didn't want me around and didn't like me. Anyway, while I was exploring *inside* the house, I got trapped and couldn't get loose. Embarrassing, huh? That's why I was determined not to let my people know about it and decided to try to work my way out by myself.

They missed me about noon. Curiously, neither of them could remember letting me out, but that didn't necessarily mean anything. As humans get older, their short term memory isn't always as accurate as you'd like it to be. They forget mealtimes and whether you're in or out and all kinds of important things. It's no fun for doggies when their humans start forgetting, I can tell you for sure. Shucks, sometimes either Master or Mistress will stop in the middle of the room or by one of the doors and ask the other in a joking manner, "What did I come in here to do?" All too often they don't remember and have to laugh at themselves and go sit back down. See what I mean? Just imagine being a little dog and having paws instead of hands so you can't do a lot of things you actually know how to but can't without having hands, and have to depend on humans. It's just one of the universe's jokes on us dogs.

Searching for me was already becoming a routine for them even as young as I was, only a few months old. Less than six, anyway. It's been a while and even my memory isn't perfect, smart as I am. They made the same rounds as before, all afternoon and into the evening. Naturally they couldn't find me because I was trapped inside the house. They even went through the house several times, calling for and checking all the closets and the storeroom and the little nooks and crannies all houses have, thinking I might have either gotten locked in a closet or caught in a tight corner or something like that, which of course I had but I wasn't going to admit it unless I absolutely had to. So they didn't find me because I wouldn't say anything and as dusk turned to darkness I was still missing. Again, they got out the big flashlights, especially the one they keep by the back door, the door that us doggies use most of the time. It has a powerful beam and is great for seeing at night. It did no good. They still couldn't find me because I wasn't outside, I was inside, still trying to wiggle loose, but it really hurt bad when I tried to go forward and I couldn't back out. At ten o'clock they grudgingly went to bed, having done everything they could think of, including searching the house from top to bottom again, looking in all the cubbyholes once more where I might have gotten locked up like the kittens frequently did when they had more than one who lived inside.

While they were in bed, my hind leg, which was what I was hung up on, had gotten so numb it no longer hurt when I moved forward. I pulled myself by my front legs and finally plopped free from the underside of that blasted chair I had gotten up into the innards of, thinking maybe a badger might try using it one day. I didn't know at the time that badgers didn't hang around in houses nor even lived in Texas, but remember how young I was then. A doggie that young can't be expected to know everything, even if he is a purebred, special dachshund like me. I was free, but my back legs were so numb I couldn't walk on them. I figured by then I ought to go ask for a little help since Master and Mistress were going to find out what happened anyway because I was bleeding. I started dragging myself toward the bedroom where they and Susie slept. Speaking of Susie, that mean dog knew where I was all the time but she never once even went near where

121

I was trapped. She wanted me to stay hung up there and die, which shows how little she cared for me, drat her hide. Anyway, dragging myself by my front feet, which are so short, is tiring. I never made it to the bedroom but I got as far as the other bathroom and drug myself in there to rest for a while.

Getting old for humans carries another handicap besides an occasional malfunction of short term memory. They have to get up and go to the bathroom a couple of times each night, or even more. Mistress got up at midnight and since she sleeps on the far side of the bed from the big bathroom, she usually uses the bathroom in the hallway at night. When she flicked on the light, there I was on the rug, looking up at her with my big brown eyes, a woebegone expression on my little floppy-eared, snuffly-nosed doggie face. Oh man, was I ever embarrassed. I lay in the puddle of a blood-soaked portion of the rug. Mistress picked me up at once and woke Master. While he held me, she followed the trail of blood and dog hair from the bathroom rug through the living room, through the kitchen and on back to the office, formerly a big two car garage. It had indoor/outdoor carpeting that was spotted with dried blood and hair over toward one corner, but she really couldn't tell where it began. Neither could Master when he tried to find where I had been, for he figured out that I had obviously gotten trapped somewhere in the office in a piece of furniture. I hated that he deduced what happened because it made me look stupid, but shucks, I was just making sure no badgers were in the house, which is what I was bred for. He should have congratulated me on doing my duty is what he should have done. Susie sure never does hers like I do!

I had a two inch long gash on my inner thigh where it had gotten hung. Master and Mistress decided that I must have crawled into the underside of the couch or into the inside of one of the big easy chairs from the bottom and gotten hung up, which was right, of course but they never did think maybe I was trying to be a big dog and go badger hunting. See what dogs get for their efforts sometimes? No credit at all. There I had stayed for twelve hours, never making a sound even when they called and called for me inside the house. Then, as they deduced, my left hind leg must have gotten so numb that I could finally force myself on past whatever obstacle was holding me without suffering a great deal of further pain. That was their explanation and, judging from the blood trail, they decided that must been what happened but they were never were able to figure out the exact chair or place inside the couch where I had become trapped. They couldn't find any blood beneath them or in the mechanical workings inside them that were open enough for a curious puppy to crawl into but naturally concealed by the seat and legs of the furniture. It was an enduring puzzle and one they never solved because I didn't start bleeding until I had pulled myself along for several yards. But they still remember and feel horrible to this day when they think of me like that, trapped and in pain for so long but never complaining aloud. They think that I must have been blaming myself for getting into the fix and that was why I never cried out or barked or responded to their calls, because I certainly knew my name by then. But you know what really aggravates me? They never once blamed Susie for not telling them where I was, and they had to know she could smell where I was. Well, I guess even if they are good, they just aren't smart enough to think of everything, but it still ticks me off the way Susie looked at that chair then looked at them then looked at me with that smug, stupid expression on her face. She ought to have been spanked is what I think.

Master and Mistress decided then and there that I was a "special needs" furry child and they thanked the heavens that people like them took me in rather than someone who wouldn't have sympathized with me or loved me and spent so much time helping me as they did. When I heard them say that, I looked at Susie and stuck out my tongue at her and wiped that smug expression off her face. Perhaps it doesn't sound like they cared that much, letting me outside by myself, but that's what made me happy, so they let me run free outside whenever I desired and I thanked them by not making them get up from their chairs so often to let me in and out like that stupid Susie does. She has no consideration for other dogs or humans either. Besides, I had already proven that I didn't even have to go outside the house to get into a world of trouble! And outside, under the big pines surrounding the house and on the tarmac of our driveway I discovered a big purpose in my life, even if my people don't quite understand it. We'll get into that eventually and I'll even show a picture of me at that purpose but in the meantime there were some other things they thought I was just going to have to learn.

THE TWO BASICS

Two of the most basic things a puppy has to learn early in life are; using the outdoors for his personal hygiene, and refraining from chasing cars or getting near their own when it is leaving or arriving. These tasks are harder to get the hang of than you might think. To begin with, where I came from was a kennel and it wasn't known for its hygiene. Basically it was a puppy breeding joint, and I'm one of the results. And cars and trucks are simply so big and noisy they are confusing to little puppies. Regardless, failure to learn the first will make for an unhappy relationship with a pup's human companions and ignoring the second might very well lead to an early and unnecessary demise, which I certainly didn't want. I didn't know at first that I had somehow acquired the ability to have more than one life, like cats, much as I hate to admit I have a similarity to them. However, without it, I wouldn't be telling this story.

I was very hard to housebreak because I had Autism and ADHD and all that and it wasn't something I felt like using my power of concentration on, and that aggravated Master and Mistress because they didn't know at first how peculiar I was. I can't see the need of going into all the details, but Susie can take part of the blame. Older dogs are supposed to teach the younger ones how to use the great outdoor rather than the confined indoors, the equivalent of the caves and immediate living environment of their wolf ancestors, but Susie didn't want me around and failed her duty on purpose, just to get me in trouble. On the other hand, Susie was separated from the only home she had ever known at about seven months, before she even entered her first heat, and still hadn't completely accepted her new home when I came along and disrupted it, so I'll give her a little bit of a break on the matter but not much. She was just contrary when I arrived on the scene and that's all there is to it.

Okay, besides Susie my humans have to take some blame as well. With the other two doggies they had let live in the house with them, they always took them quite a ways out into the yard to show them where to do their business. For some reason, they didn't go nearly as far with me, maybe because Susie was barking at the moon or imaginary boogers or something and distracted them. I can't even remember the real reason now. Perhaps they didn't take me way out because of my problems navigating the steps, even after Master fixed them so I could go up and down, but they still were causing me problems because I always saw two or three when there was really only one there. Also I think they became impatient because once I was outside with them to protect me I had more things on my mind than peeing or pooping. At any rate, when I finally did get the idea I wasn't supposed to go inside the house, I used the porch as often as not or the brick sidewalk leading from the front to the back where the cars are parked. I just hated going up and down those stupid steps when I couldn't see them clearly. They thought I was a slow learner so I hope now I've dispelled that notion for you. My people can look back now and think, *Well of course. He was raised in a kennel and we didn't get him until he was almost eight weeks old. At the kennel he had to go on the cement floor, right near where he slept.* Sure. And dadgum it, once I get something fixed in my little one-track mind, I just don't like to have to change things around. I have other things to do, you know, which I'll get to.

A little sidebar. Even when I was very young, I was so fixated on doing things my own way that my people began to jokingly refer to me as having only two brain cells and rarely has them both working at the same time. It's still sort of a joke, but not nearly as funny since they can now sympathize with me. It's just the way my little doggie mind is wired. If I seem odd, it's because I do things my own way. And if I goof, well, I have as many lives as a cat, don't I? Dumb cats. How did they get so lucky? That's probably it. They just lucked out getting so many lives when evolution was getting going. They're so dumb they couldn't have done it themselves, that's for sure.

At any rate, I do use the outdoors almost all the time. Occasionally in the middle of the night I will go to the bedroom and if Master or Mistress doesn't hear me scratching on the rug on one side of the bed or the other at once (usually Mistress' side since she's easier to wake up), I will pee there just to teach them not to be so slow waking up and paying attention to me—then continue scratching to wake up the person on whichever side of the bed I'm on so they get the lesson right then. Humans are hard to train and it's best to reinforce their lessons at once so they learn faster.

Outside, if I go out in the morning before daylight, about half the time I will poop on the porch. Heck, how would you like it if you had to squat out in the dark and not know what you were squatting over? Derned if I'm going to let a bug or even a snake bite my hind end just because I can't see good, especially at night. I guess I will always pee on the porch part of the time because of Pat & Rob's dog Browine, who always stops and leaves his mark on a corner post in passing. I have to make my mark to go over his and obliterate it so in case another dog comes along they will know a purebred dachshund lives there and not some stupid mongrel. The humans know this and they can't blame me for that, especially since it's a big porch and varmints wander up onto it at night sometimes looking for scraps of food, or if the humans have been careless and left a chair near the table where Velcro the Cat eats they'll use it to climb up on the table and polish off anything left in the three bowls there. That brings up a pet gripe of mine. I don't mind if they feed Velcro on the table (although I wouldn't be caught dead eating cat food anyway. They put it up there to protect it from Susie, who will eat anything that doesn't move), but why do they leave his bowl up there so I can't polish it. I won't eat cat food, of course, but I like to see clean bowls on the porch. Clean bowls show that a good dog lives at the place and keeps them polished, but how can I polish Velcro's bowl when they leave it up on the table? The dumb cat sure won't do it. They're so dumb they don't know how. And speaking of Velcro, if we have to have a cat around to keep the mice and frog population under control, I suppose Velcro will do as well as any. A cat is a cat as far as I'm concerned, except for some cats that are mean.

All in all, for an autistic, ADHD affected doggie, I guess I don't do that bad. On some of Master's dachshund groups he reads about dogs that never do get housebroken, or revert at times. They're satisfied with how I do now and know I try my best, given my handicaps—which I haven't finished listing yet! Any time I have an accident you can be sure it's because I had more important things on my mind than fooling with steps that seem to multiply every time I look at them. My darned eyes just won't focus right.

Oh yes, one more thing; a funny for you. As I matured, like all boy dogs, I began to cock my hind leg when I peed. This is how male dogs mark their territory and also how they leave "notes" to each other, such as *I was here about three days ago* or *I am about this high*. Raising the leg and getting their stream as high as they can on the surface of whatever they are marking is simply a means of telling other dogs how big they are, among other information. It takes a little practice to get it right, just like a baby learning to walk. At first when I began cocking my hind leg, I fell over as often as not, like a lot of clumsy pups do. But Master and Mistress never stopped to think it might have been because of the injury to my hind leg when I was trapped in that pesky chair that caused me to fall over and still causes problems. Eventually I got the hang of it

126

except for one thing: Because of that scar on my hind leg, I can't aim worth a flip. As often as not I wind up peeing on my own chest instead of on what I'm aiming for. Can you imagine how embarrassing that is for a purebred Dachshund Doggie? I bet Master really feels guilty while he's typing this right now for thinking I was just too dumb to aim straight when it is that injury that causes me to pee on my chest.

So far as the cars go, I have never cared for them, or trucks either, unless they belonged to us, and even then I don't like them much exept for the interesting smells they pick up when they go somewhere. Sometimes they even come back with a doggie mark on them from far off, which teaches me a little about geography and what another town is like and so on, so they do have their uses I have to admit. They had no problem at all with me staying out of the way of visitors coming and going because why should I care where they've been or what they've done, but our vehicles are a different matter. I was scared of them at first, just like I was of others since I can't see them too well, but once I learned which car and truck belonged to us, I came about as close as I ever would to dying. Heck, I may even have died and used up one of those cat lives for all I know.

First, Master's truck. By the time I arrived he had already closed the Christmas tree farm, so he used the truck only to go to the mailbox and to go for the paper. Occasionally, he would drive into our little town a few miles away to haul off trash or to fill the truck with gas, but basically it's just for running around the farm and as an emergency backup vehicle in case the car is gone wherever cars go when they aren't here and I'm in trouble and they have to use it to take me to see Dr. Bob. Our home is about a third of a mile down our private gravel road from the county blacktop where our mailbox is and where the paper is delivered each morning, or so Master says. I've never been that far myself because he gets angry if I try to go that way. I guess he's scared I'll get lost again and he'll have to wander around in the woods again at night with that flashlight looking for me. It's the only reason I know.

Back behind our house and on the other side of our private road is the home of Pat and Rob, their daughter and son-in-law. Follow the road on back for another half mile and it dead ends at son Mike and daughter-in-law Linda's home. Our home and Rob & Pat's are less than a hundred yards or so from each other, but separated by a tree line on each side of our road. Also, behind our house and on our side of the road, also separated by a tree line, is where the garden lives. All these homes are surrounded by trees, mostly pines, which means the ground is usually covered with brown pine straw, a perfect camouflage for "red" dachsunds like me—although I'm more black on my back then red. Red dachshunds and pine straw are almost the same color.

I've described the layout of the farm and homes and the surroundings so that you can understand how easy it would be for someone to run over a little reddish brown dachshund puppy. When I first began associating Master with the truck I didn't try to follow him up to the county blacktop road, but I learned the sound of it well enough to know it was him coming back. The problem was, Rob was taking a morning paper at the time, so when Master went up to get his paper he picked up Rob's, too. He would drive on past our house and cut into their yard, throw his paper, then swing back around by the garden and come back home through the little side lane there. That annoyed the pee out of me because I expected him to just come on home and see me after getting the paper. I mean after all, who's more important, some dumb son-in-law or a real pureblood dachshund puppy? It's no contest, is it? Of course I'm the most important and he should come directly home first before giving Rob his paper. I may not can see good but I can hear well enough, and I learned the route by the sound of the truck and thought it was great fun to try to outrun the truck by taking short cuts through the little game trails cutting through the two tree lines separating our house from theirs, or the tree line separating our house from the garden, just to show Master I was more important than Rob. The first time he saw my little brown figure dart in front of the truck he almost had a heart attack because he came so close to running over me. he had to stop the truck for a moment to regain his breath and slow down his heart rate before continuing on, which is what I intended for him to do—stop and look at me instead of fooling around delivering Rob's paper. After he started up again without paying attention to me, I would go again, running like crazy and not even paying attention to things I couldn't see like spider webs and stuff. I would cut back through the tree line and again almost get hit when I ran in front of the truck in the lane from the garden on the way back to the house. By golly, I was determined to put a stop to that detour he took in the morning.

Master shouted at me. He stopped the truck and ran me home instead of patting me so I just went back again, going back through the same routine again, trying to teach Master what he was supposed to do. He was hard to train sometimes. I've mentioned that, haven't I? Sometimes I made him have to stop three times on that hundred yard route between our house and Rob and Pat's. Once Master got the idea it was a game, there seemed no way to get it out of his mind. He just knew he would hit me one day, even though he made certain to drive

128

slow every time he got back near the house from the county road in the truck. He tried disciplining me when he could catch me running after or trying to outwit Truck, hard as it was when I looked up at him with that goofy, happy expression, telling him what fun me and him and Truck just had, even if he didn't learn much. Mistress tried disciplining me, too. Master even spanked me, something she couldn't bring herself to do. Nothing seemed to help. I just couldn't get them trained and I was really getting aggravated that Master and Mistress were acting so dumb over the truck business, almost dumb as a cat, which is sure no compliment!

At the same time, I began expressing an interest in the car. I can't smell too good, but it did always have some different odors on its round paws (and I still don't see how Car or Truck walks or runs with those things). I wasn't interested in outwitting the car like I was with Master and the truck but I did decide to try following Car and see where it went to get those lovely smells of dead possum and chewing gum and fresh dirt and cookie crumbs and stuff by following it as Mistress or Master, or both of them, left to go somewhere in it. One thing Master absolutely did not want me to learn about was the existence of the county road. He didn't realize how well I could hear and I already knew there had to be a road up there just from the sound of other cars and trucks going up and down it on their round paws. Master thought I was so idiotic that it wouldn't take long at all for me to get run over for sure if I ever started going up there, and I didn't know how to tell him I wasn't interested in those other cars and trucks but just wanted to see where our car went. So when I began trying to follow the car, Master thought he had to get really tough. Sometimes he would stop or they would stop four or five times while leaving while he got out and chased me back home. Again he thought it was a game and I couldn't teach him it wasn't any better than I could with the truck. Master and Mistress seem to have a blind spot in their brains over the matter of me wanting to find out where they take the car. They simply wouldn't allow it to go on, me following the car, because they expected me not to live very much longer if it did. They didn't know I had as many lives as a cat. The next three times I tried to follow the car, Master got out and chased me back home. He went all the way and gave me a spanking that was not hard enough to hurt me physically but did hurt my feelings, and each time he repeated over and over "Stay! Stay home!" like it was a mantra or something, so I finally decided since he and Mistress couldn't be trained about me wanting to know where the car went to get those good smells, I just gave up on them - so far as doing it openly.

Then I waited until I thought the car was out of sight (an easy mistake for me to make with my stupid crossed eyes) and began running up the road after it. Unfortunately, Master caught me both times I tried before getting to the county road and gave my little backside a tanning, not really hurting me but certainly letting me know he thought I had been bad when really it was him just being so dumb. Not only that, he began taking me with him in the truck up to the road and back. The old truck, bought new in 1984, was over twenty years old and rattled and banged like a covered wagon. Being inside it scared me to death because I couldn't see where all the noises were coming from.

The two actions together seemed to my people to work, when actually I just gave up trying to train them. They were hopeless about their car and truck. From then on I might follow the car to where the driveway tarmac ends, but that was it. All I could do was stare wistfully at it leaving and imagine it going out and rubbing itself over stuff to get those good smells. And, amazingly, Master thought I seemed to connect both the car and truck with the idea I wasn't to get near them while they were moving. Naturally since I couldn't teach him any better, I quit chasing and cutting through the tree lines after the truck, trying to outwit it by getting to Rob's house first or back home first. When he takes the truck to the garden now, I will still follow, but at a sedate pace and wait until it is safely stopped before approaching. They could finally rest easy, but to this day, they are both very careful. When they leave or come back, they make certain I'm not in the way. It sure is a shame he couldn't learn because I never have got to find out where Car finds all those good smells.

CUTIE PIE, VELCRO AND THE PORCH

My people have been living out here on the farm for almost thirty years now and stayed here even after closing the Christmas tree farm simply because they love it. I don't blame them. I love living here, too, with all the things there are to do to keep me busy and happy, not like old couch potato Susie who won't bestir herself unless she imagines there's something around to bark at, which she does about twenty dozen times a day. The house has a porch. For almost all of the last eighteen years there was only one boss of the porch, regardless of the other dogs who lived with them and slept on the porch in all but the very coldest weather. They were big dogs usually, who liked to roam the countryside, got very dirty and muddy and simply weren't the type for inside living like us dachshunds are. Of course we're purebred, which makes a difference. Anyway, the boss of the porch was Cutie Pie. Cutie Pie, a cat bossing the porch, would you believe? She wasn't even intended to be their cat. They kept her from one of the litters back when they still had mother cats for their daughter, Colleen, who lives farther west in Texas. Unfortunately, Colleen became involved in moving and other things and was never able come see them and pick up her cat until Cutie Pie had already been named. That happened by continuing to refer to her as a cutie pie since she was so adorable looking as a kitten. Shucks, even I have to admit kittens are kind of cute. Not as cute as puppies, of course, and not even adorable like they said, but cute. Before they knew it, she had made a home with them. She lived on the porch and grew up to be a big mean cat and bossed the porch from then on.

Cutie Pie never did like inside living so that's why they let her have her own way. Personally, I just think she likes it on the porch because she can be boss there when inside the house she couldn't. Anyway, my people's first addition to the home they built when they first moved out here was a huge roofed front porch with an uncovered side deck extending almost all the way to the back where Car and Truck live. That was also near the back door where most people who know us come and go. Near the front door leading to the porch they kept a succession of reinforced cardboard boxes in a little alcove they lined with old blankets and rugs for Cutie Pie, which is good enough for her I think—but woe to the dog who tried to take her space! In fact woe to the puppy who didn't bow to her authority right off the bat. She let them know right quick with a swat of her clawed right paw that she owned the porch and other animals were allowed to use it only on her sufferance. I told you she was mean, didn't I?

I did manage to learn that one thing quickly. Two swats by Cutie Pie and I admitted she owned the porch. Shucks, I didn't want the porch anyway, except to pee on when it's raining or to over-pee after Brownie has peed on it. All that pee keeps Mistress washing it often for some reason. I don't know why, it just gets peed on again. Anyway, Cutie Pie had to allow us dogs to come and go and even reinforce Brownie's marks on the big iron table legs or corner posts but it took a while before she let me approach her in a friendly manner. She was a very tough old cat as the Veterinary Hospital learned when my people took her in for neutering. She escaped and they had to call for a lock down. Once she was fixed, the hospital people were very glad not to have anything further to do with her. Did I mention how mean she was?

Velcro the cat came along a year or so before Susie and me arrived. He is a pretty cat - for a cat, that is - with a nose of four distinct colors. He lived inside the house until he was almost grown but unfortunately he was unable to learn that Mistress' kitchen counters were not a place for kitty cats to play. He finally had to be relegated to the porch to live with Cutie Pie, which was fine with me. I wouldn't want to live in a house with a cat anyway. They aren't refined enough in my opinion.

I eventually learned that Velcro would play with me (and I was forced to play with a *cat* because Susie wouldn't play) but despite all my efforts, Cutie Pie remained aloof. She was not a playful cat; she had a porch to run.

Besides, she was too mean to play, I think.

MONSTERS AND NIGHTMARES

My world is inhabited by monsters. Master and Mistress have no way of knowing now what went on at the kennel, where I was the runt of the litter. They're sure I must have had a hard time there and they're right. Kennel's aren't very happy places to begin with and the dogs are kept penned up like they've committed a crime of some kind and never given treats and have to pee in their own home if they can't wait and bad people sometimes buy the puppies and on and on. Yeah, kennel life was tough for a little guy like me. I had to take whatever was left at dinner time and the bigger dogs picked on me all the time and teased me because I couldn't see good and made life miserable for me there. But some of my experiences since coming to live with Master and Mistress have been horrible for a young puppy as well, even though none of them were their fault. Things just happen sometimes for no good reason unless maybe a cat is behind them. Cats are untrustworthy and you have to keep your eye on them.

I began having nightmares from all the bad things that have happened to me, where I will suddenly let out a terrible defensive growl, as if preparing to fight for my life, which in the dream is certainly true. Sometimes it's a huge old bobcat, or a pack of raunchy mangy coyotes after me or a vacuum cleaner monster grown to gigantic size trying to suck me up into its belly or…well, just bad dreams, okay? I will wake from a sound sleep doing that barking and growling, hair bristling along the nape of my neck like cactus spikes, and ready to fight whatever it was in the dream. But mostly I growl, at something I obviously just dreamed about, and it startles my people. After waking up I will look around, totally confused at first that I am not being threatened. When I realize I'm in my own bed in the living room, I get sort of a guilty expression on my doggie face, as if saying, *Whoops! That wasn't real, was it?*

They have no way of knowing what my dreams are about, but they think they must be bad. Perhaps it's the thunder monsters or the 18 wheeler monsters or the pain monster that visits after a snake bite is what they think, and yet they laugh at my reaction anyway. Like they

133

don't have bad dreams themselves. I know, I've heard Master screaming at night from his PTSD he got in the war and Mistress dreams about a booger chasing her just like I do. But I'm more refined than humans so I don't laugh at them when they dream. Any number of things are possible, but to me they're all monsters when I wake up growling. Besides that, I'm scared of anything left out of place, or new things added to the habitat, like a new chair on the porch or a different couch. I'm afraid of strange cars or tractors, sudden movements, the lawn tractor and innumerable other objects and events, too many to list, but it's all because I can't see well and don't know whether the things are good are bad.

My people usually refer to the things I'm scared of sort of jokingly, although they're pretty sure it's not a joke to me and they're slap dab right about that! One of them will say, "You'd better leave the room, Tonto. The vacuum cleaner monster is coming," or, "Aw, are those thunder boogers scaring our baby? C'mon, you can sit in my lap." This last one is no joke at all. I really am terrified of thunder monsters and insist on being held in a lap while it's happening. I want someone bigger than me by my side if the thunder monsters ever decide to come down the chimney after us. As bad as they sound they must look horrible! Master and Mistress are surprised that I'm such a happy little dog other than the times the boogers or monsters are after me, but then they will remember I live in my own little world, like autistic human pups do.

MY UNIQUE ABILITIES

When I was about six months old or thereabouts, Master and Mistress began to see the ADHD and/or Autism syndrome come into play. This involved my almost total devotion to sticks and my use of them. It also showed that I am a very intelligent dog in my own way. Of course purebred dachshunds are naturally very intelligent, but I have a different kind. I'm special. In fact, I am the only dog they have ever even heard of that not only uses a tool for a specific purpose, but actually creates them if necessary! Now if that's not being pretty darned smart I don't know what is!

As I've said before, our house is surrounded by big pines, which naturally means a lot of fallen branches. At first Master and Mistress noticed me simply playing with sticks, as they call the smaller branches I use. I was playing with them because lazy old Susie wouldn't play and Velcro wasn't interested in the same things I was. He wanted me to roll around in the dust with him and go (shiver!) snake hunting, so we didn't play together that much. Anyway, I started to go out under the pine trees, find me a fallen branch about a foot or two long and carry it around in my mouth. When I get tired of that stick, I'd go find another one and another and another, spending hours at this game. The people didn't know what to make of it, of course, but I had my own reasons for playing with sticks. What I was doing wasn't really play; it just looked like it; I was really using sticks to mark paths outside so I would remember where I had been and know how to find places again. I can't see good and can't smell very well either, so I use sticks to make reference points. The bad thing is, my people don't understand and keep picking them up and using them to start fires with or just making piles of them to keep them away from the Lawn tractor monster they let loose for it to get some exercise every now and then. If you want my opinion, they could keep the blamed thing locked up in the car port all the time. In fact, I don't know what they keep a monster like that around to begin with, but I'm getting off the subject.

We have an asphalt driveway that extends well beyond the area where they park Car and Truck (since the carport was filled up with other stuff about ten seconds after being built). It is partially overhung by a few of the pines, so much of the time it is covered with pine straw. We also have big bay windows in the office, which Master and Mistress expanded from a two car garage. From them, we can look out on the back yard, the driveway, and the treelines beyond. One day, Master was in the office and went to the back of the room for a book. He looked out beyond the cars and saw me on the asphalt drive doing something with a stick that I seemed to be holding in an odd position. He couldn't quite figure out what I was up to, so he quietly opened the door and went a little closer to me. Incredibly (to him), I was holding one end of a twelve inch stick in my mouth with the rest of it sticking straight out in front of me. I was using the stick in such a position that I could walk along and watch the other end of it scraping along the asphalt, making little piles of the pine straw that covered it! Once I got my technique down, I spent hours out with my sticks, shoveling pine straw into little hillocks. Master and Mistress didn't have a clue why I was doing it for or what I got out of it, so they thought it was just a manifestation of me being autistic, and to a degree I guess it is. However, I have another purpose. What I'm doing is clearing the tarmac of copperhead snakes. They are the same color as straw and like to conceal themselves in it. The tarmac is my territory and I sure don't want those evil things around, but I don't want to get too close to them, either. And of course you know I can't see well. The rest should be easy to understand, but I'll tell just in case someone exceptionally dumb is reading this. The sticks pushing the straw is a means of scaring the snakes away from the tarmac while not getting close enough for one of them to bite me. Simple, huh? After that first snake bite, I sure didn't want another one and so I figured out a way to keep them away from me. I don't know why it's so hard for humans to understand something so simple but then they aren't purebred dachshunds, either, so maybe that explains it.

The sticks have to be the proper length. I discovered through experimentation that about eight to twelve inches was the best length for my purpose. I will use one for a while then, according to Master, tire of it for some reason and go hunt up another, bring it back, and start shoveling pine straw again. Actually, I haven't gotten tired of it. I just decided to use it to mark where I had already been and go get another one. Doing that gives me a little bit of a break and lets me know where I've been—if Car or Truck doesn't run over them or Master or Mistress pick them up because they think they're in the way. I wish I could have explained why I left them, but they didn't understand when I yelped and woofed and tried to tell them.

As I continued with this self-appointed task, and spent so much time at it, Master and Mistress began telling each other when I asked to go out, "Well, Tonto is going to work." I guess I was, after a fashion. I concentrated on it in typical ADHD or Autistic fashion, doing little else for hours at a time. I sure didn't want those copperheads to bite me and for that matter, even if they didn't know it, I was protecting Master and Mistress from copperheads, too!

This wasn't the end of it though, not by any means. As I learned the various aspects of my job, I discovered that it was fun to see how fast I could go with the stick held out in front of me, piling up the pine straw. I can't see any reason in the world not to make work fun, if you can. Shucks, Master works at writing, but he says it's fun and Mistress works in the yard, but she says it's fun. See? Anyway, soon I was actually *running* like that, from one end of the asphalt to the other. It was kind of dangerous because I might have run into a copperhead by going so fast, so my people thought, but they never noticed that I didn't start the running until I had pretty well made sure the copperheads had all been scared away already. Every time they saw me going so fast they cringed, thinking any moment the end of the stick would get hung up on the asphalt and cause the other end being held in my mouth to be rammed forcefully down my throat. It never happened though, because part of my trouble with chewing also gives me such a firm grip with my jaws that something like that could never happen. I don't know why humans are such slow thinkers or so unintelligent they can't figure things like that out. Maybe they aren't purebred like us dachshunds are. It's the only reason I can think of. Anyway, I hold those sticks out in front of me and down to the tarmac in my jaws with an iron grip! And actually, the asphalt is much smoother than they think it is. I really don't have a problem at all and I soon dispelled the notion that I might by expanding my territory.

After piling all the straw on the driveway into little heaps with my sticks, and scaring away snakes in the process, I began to move out into the pine straw that mingled with the mown grass on either side of it. There, my humans *knew* the surface wasn't smooth, yet never once have they seen my stick hang up. Finally they quit worrying about it, as well they should have. Their suspicions that I must be able to sense the exact distance the tip of my stick is from whatever surface I'm shoveling the straw on is exactly right and it's the only explanation they can think of, anyway. It is just another part of me being special and different from other dogs, although purebred dachshunds are always pretty smart.

Remember I said I was a tool-using dog? I certainly am, just as much as a man using a hammer to drive nails is a tool-using human, but I went further than that. My next step was actually *making* my tool! I don't know why Master and Mistress think it's so unusual. After all, I am a purebred dachshund and I have special talents besides. It's no big thing, actually. I could invent lots of ways to make and use tools if I wanted to. They watched me one day as we all wandered out under the pine trees one morning while I was looking for a stick of the proper length to begin my day's work of shoveling straw, as Master and Mistress thought, and scaring away copperhead snakes as I was actually doing. Unfortunately, Master had picked up the larger dry branches to use as kindling for the Franklin stove and had let the Mower Monster loose under the pine trees the day before, something he'd only do once every couple of months since the pine straw keeps the grass and weeds pretty well at bay in that area. This all made it to where I couldn't find a stick of the proper length. The only one I was able to locate that came even close to suiting me was about two feet long. Later on I would figure out a use for those, too, but right then I was intent on shoveling straw to scare away the snakes for the day and was stymied for lack of the right stick. Finally, while they were still watching me, I took one of the longer sticks and chewed it into two pieces, thereby creating two sticks of the proper length, each about a foot long. Nonchalantly, I picked one of them up by the end, got a good grip on it and went happily about my business, shoveling the straw and scaring snakes. I don't know why the humans got so excited about something so simple that they ran and got the camera and took pictures of me at work. Well, I shouldn't complain because pictures of a purebred dachshund at work are appropriate and enticing to look at for any human.

They took a picture the next time they saw me doing this, too. On the back cover of the book is a picture of me shoveling straw to scare copperheads away. You can clearly see the marks on my stick where I have chewed it to the right length for working. Master queried some dog groups and dachshund groups about this behavior and no one has ever heard of a dog who has gone to such lengths (no pun intended) to satisfy his desire to perform a specific task, but all I have to say about that is that it just shows I'm a special dog and a purebred dachshund to boot and Master was perfectly right to choose me as the avatar for his novel *Bark!* No other dachshund dog would have fit.

There is a variation of shoveling and scaring snakes that I eventually discovered and decided I liked, both for a little variety at work and because I was then able to use the longer branches for it, even the forked ones. In fact, a lot of the time I prefer the forked variety as the year wears on and the snakes get bigger. Instead of shoveling straw to scare them, I found that I enjoyed sweeping the straw into piles and it scared them even better since they were sort of getting used to the plain old stick shoveling. In this case, I held one end of his branch sideways in my mouth rather than straight out in front of me. Then I would get on the driveway or in the grass and turn in circles, sweeping the straw. It looked as if I enjoyed holding one of the forks of my sticks in this fashion, so I could not only see part of it sweeping up straw and scaring copperheads, but could watch the other part moving in the circle with me. I can't see a thing wrong with adding a little fun to work. Humans ought to try it more often themselves and maybe they wouldn't be so grouchy.

I actually enjoy my job so much and Master and Mistress liked watching me so much that even after it would rain and wash most of the straw off the driveway they got into the habit of keeping some straw in big plastic trash bags, and when they thought I needed more dry straw to work with they would simply empty a bag or two of it onto the driveway for me until the pine trees had shed enough to give me fresh straw to work with. They didn't realize that I could have taken a few days off from work with a clean driveway since snakes couldn't hide on it, but I don't hold it against them. Anyway, there was still the rest of the back yard that had to be kept snake free so I couldn't have taken that much time off anyway.

I get so exasperated when Master gets out the wheelbarrow because I know right then he's going to go out and pick up all the sticks I've very carefully put down for markers so I know where I am all the time. I always follow him around and try to grab the sticks before he can get to them, but it's like he's got a magic eye or something. He is also bigger and faster at grabbing sticks than me so he always gets them, and then I have to start leaving my markers under the pine trees all over again. Master sure makes it hard on a little short legged dachshund, even though he really doesn't know how much trouble he's causing me. Sometimes I guess a pup just has to put up with the things their humans do. I even try to fool him by finding sticks that have just fallen and substituting them for the ones I've put down, but he just winds up taking them both. I will say he does very carefully thank me for my sticks when he puts them in the wheel barrow but it would be nicer if he just left them alone. Oh well. I'm eating so much these days I need the exercise anyway. And if anyone wants a little dachshund's opinion, most humans could use a little more exercise themselves!

The only real problem with me and my sticks is that sometimes when I get tired I'll lay down with a stick and begin gnawing on it. If I don't go to sleep, I have to stay busy, not like some lazy dogs and cats that live around here I could name. I like to keep my mind occupied and sharp so I don't turn into a couch potato like Susie, or sleep my life away like Velcro or Cutie Pie did before she died. Unfortunately, when I'm gnawing on a stick, invariably the bark gets to tasting pretty good and sometimes even the wood is kind of tasty and I chew it up and eat it. Sticks don't really sit very well in a doggie's tummy, so every time I eat a stick or chew the bark off one eventually I will barf it up. Fortunately for Mistress, she insisted on changing over to hardwood floors before I came to live with them so it's no great problem, and I've gradually learned that when I start gagging it's time to head for the nearest door. I get fooled more often than not though because I always gag after drinking water for some reason I've never figured out. I should amend that to say the humans get fooled. I've pretty well learned to recognize and differentiate the water gag and the stick gag, but they can't. Maybe they're just not smart enough.

ANOTHER SNAKE BITES ME

My poor eyesight, and possibly my poor sense of smell, got me into trouble with a snake again shortly before I was grown and thought I had scared them all off. I can hear perfectly well but, unfortunately, snakes don't make much noise. One day, several months after my first snake bite, but before this other bite I'm going to tell you about, Master heard Susie's shrill, short, yelping snake bark. By this time he and Mistress had learned to recognize it. She barks a lot, but her snake bark is so distinctive they have no trouble identifying it. But she barks so dern much that I got in the habit of mostly ignoring her so I failed to think what she might be barking at. Naturally, I happened to be outside with her.

My humans hurried out, with Master grabbing the hoe as he went since Mistress is scared of snakes, even harmless little six foot chicken snakes. They were just in time to see an almost unbelievable act. I walked right *over* the snake that Susie was barking at. It was a non-poisonous variety but even some of those can give little doggies a nasty bite. The snake was about three feet long and was attempting to make a getaway when I stepped over it as it slithered along. I never even noticed it was there, even though I knew Susie was barking at something but, like I said, she barks all the time anyway so who wants to pay attention to that? I think that was the final confirmation for my humans that I was indeed cross-eyed. I can see, but as Dr. Bob told them, he has no idea of *what* I see. He also told them there were tests that could determine the extent of my impaired vision, but that we were better off not spending the money since there was little to be done for it in any case. I thought that was kind of idiotic reasoning but he's the vet so I didn't argue with him and neither did my people.

If seeing me step over the snake wasn't enough to make believers of my people, their plumber confirmed it. I like to hang around wherever any kind of work is going on to make sure it's being done right, like a good dog should. On this particular day, the plumber asked them about my vision when I almost fell into the hole that the commode normally covered, because I saw two of them and thought

141

the wrong one was the real one. It was open while the plumber was doing some work. He picked me up and brought me back out to them and asked if I had vision problems. That gave them a good laugh, because of course I have. I thought it was sort of mean for the plumber to make an issue of it, though. I wonder if he would have done that to a human pup?

Back to my second snake bite. My people didn't see this one. I was outside late in the evening, working at my regular job of shoveling or sweeping straw, they thought, because they still didn't know I was doing that to scare snakes away and protecting not only me but Master and Mistress too, when one of them decided to step outside for some fresh air. Just about the same time, I came limping up. I hadn't even seen that damn snake. It had been hiding and ambushed me, probably taking revenge for all the times I'd scared it away. A quick examination told Maser and Mistress the cause. I had been bitten again, on the foreleg this time, probably from stepping on a copperhead in the pine straw under the trees where they blend in so well they are well nigh invisible. That's what they thought, and that's just about how it happened. Damn, those bites hurt!

This happened so late that Dr. Bob's office was closed. My people left a message that was supposed to go to his cell phone, but he had forgotten to take it out of his truck after a service call and hadn't missed it, which was kind of stupid of him if you ask me. I may be addled but if I had hands to use a phone I bet I wouldn't forget it. Or maybe I would if it was in a truck. I don't like trucks anyway. Fortunately, they had some pain pills left over from my previous snakebite and I didn't feel like putting up much of a fuss when Master stuffed one down my throat. Once one of those was down home, they put me to bed with them so they could watch me close. Neither Susie nor me was sleeping with them by then for good reasons, but they made an exception that time, particularly since their calls to a backup vet also went unanswered. The next morning, I was so sore and hurt so much I could barely walk. We were first ones at Dr. Bob's Animal Hospital that day. I got a shot for pain, which I like a lot better than those darn pills, a shot of steroids again, and more antibiotics and pain pills. Within a day or so the only remaining symptom was difficulty with elimination. I fell over every time I tried to cock my sore leg and really had a hard time with the other business. Master and Mistress laughed at me, but by golly, I'd like to see them try cocking a leg that's been snakebit and see if they laugh then! I got over it though, and seemed none the worse for the experience. I think I was getting immune to the copperhead venom by then.

142

I CAN'T JUMP & CAN'T SIT UP

Biscuit, my humans' previous dachshund, was so well coordinated and intelligent that they never had to teach him to sit up. From the time he was a puppy, he spent half his life sitting up on his hinny so he could get a better view of things around him. They said his front paws were free so much of the time he used them almost like hands, by gesturing with them and touching them to get their attention and so on. He could even sit up in a moving car, balancing perfectly even on bumpy roads, or while going around curves and when the car took off and stopped. Sitting up came so naturally to Biscuit that Master honestly believed it was a dachshund trait while he was alive, built into their genes in order to enable them to see more of the world since we are so short, but it ain't so. Biscuit was just a natural athlete, and pretty smart besides, like all dachshunds, of course.

Susie and me dispelled the notion that dachshunds can naturally sit up because they've been unable to teach either of us to sit up like Biscuit did. That's because Susie is too lazy to sit when she can lay, and I have more problems to worry about than spending my time sitting up like a trained idiot dog in a circus. Susie can at least jump, surprisingly well for having such short legs, the shortest I've ever seen on a dachshund. She manages to get herself up on the couch or any chair in the house with no difficulty at all. She was able to raise her body and put her front paws on objects or people from the time they got her when she was seven months old.

I just can't jump at all—or perhaps I could, but I'm always so scared of where I'll land because of my poor vision. The highest they've ever seen me jump is less than six inches, and it took me over two years to figure out the real distances so I could raise up and put my front paws on the edge of the chairs when I want their attention for something. Outside, when I run to them when they call from the porch (if I don't' have something more important to do) and I try to jump the five or six inches at its lowest end, I frequently misjudge and fall short, bumping my head into the vertical plank that seals the underside of the porch from varmints. It ticks the heck out of me, too. I get tired of

143

bumping my head all the time. It's no wonder I have problems thinking sometimes. I have to be very careful going up and down the steps, even after I learned to negotiate them, and I still prefer the short end of the porch where Master put a couple of bricks which enables me to take a short step before reaching the deck of the porch.

Sometimes I blame that first flying leap from Master's chair for my problems, but Dr. Bob told me it isn't that. I just can't see well and when I get in a hurry, or have my mind on other things like monsters or boogers or things that go bump in the night, I'm likely to misjudge distances, even well known ones. It's just part of my life by now and I know I have to put up with it.

Another problem is getting down from chairs or the couch if Master or Mistress forgets and leaves me there. I'm not about to try jumping down when I can't tell which floor is the real one and which is an illusion. I bet you wouldn't either, would you? Occasionally I'll be letting Master or Mistress share one or the other big easy chairs with me and they'll get up for a moment, and then decide to do something else, completely forgetting that they've left me on the chair. The edge of the easy chair is too high for me to trust myself in jumping down. I just won't do it, even after Master has shown me that I can by easing me off the edge, but I don't have a choice then because he's so much bigger than me and can shove me off if he wants to, abusive or not. Mistress' chair is lower and I would probably attempt to get down from it by myself except for one thing—it rocks when I stand up and approach the edge, which makes the floor seem like there's three of them and I don't know which is which. That makes me too uneasy to attempt the jump down. The couch is a different matter. After about two and a half years, I can finally get down from the couch by myself, albeit nervously. I would *much* rather someone help me down.

I know what the problem is with me not sitting up. I don't want to. I think it looks silly and I don't intend to do it. Master never spent much time trying to teach Susie since she can get up on couches and chairs, but he has tried with me, despite me showing him plain as anything I'm not interested. He thinks I'm doing it wrong, and he never has gotten the idea I just don't want to. I finally convinced him to give up and after that I decided to teach him a few things to give him a little exercise and keep him from worrying about me being a little peculiar.

FETCHING

One day I decided to see if Master could be taught to toss an object for me to fetch. Maybe it was because he saw I had already learned to carry sticks around (even if I did hold them in a peculiar way), but he caught on to the trick of tossing quickly, surprising me because he's usually kind of a slow learner. I used a hard rubber squeaky toy for Master's lessons. Since I am so suspicious of treats and will *never* take one from a hand until I have first examined one on the floor, I couldn't use treats as a teaching tool like you can for most humans. It didn't seem to matter, though. Since my seeing and my sense of smell is impaired, maybe it was the very distinct noise this toy made that attracted me to it and made me decide to use it for Master's lessons. The very first time I began playing with him and this toy, my little head jerked up so fast it made my ears flop and got his attention real quick. When I brought him the toy, sure enough, he tossed it right off and I ran to fetch it so I could reinforce the lesson before he forgot what he was tossing it for. It took only a few attempts, with him squeaking it then throwing it a couple of feet then gradually extending the distance, and he had the trick down pat. Pretty fast learning for a human, I thought. Maybe he's not all that dumb. The toy's squeak isn't the kind that most dogs can gnaw out of the toy in a few seconds, like Biscuit always did—he was convinced the squeaks were little varmints and killed them quickly. Even Biscuit would have had a hard time killing the squeak in this one. It is well embedded in the hard rubber so it can't be chewed out, and I didn't want to anyway since Master enjoys tossing it around so much.

Once Master learned the trick, he had no problem at all extending it to other toys. Whatever I fetched, he would throw. He will toss toys for hours if I let him, with me running and fetching them for him and bringing them back, continuing the game until he is exhausted. He would probably toss toys all day if he could keep it up. The only exception is sticks. I think I've taught him by now that sticks are something special. They are tools, not to be treated like toys. Throw a stick and I may go get it but I won't bring it back. I will take it somewhere else and place it down for later use as a tool or as a marker, like sticks should be used for.

While I've got sticks in the subject, I can tell another story about them. Sometimes I will decide, for reasons unknown to my people, that it might be a good idea to store some sticks in out of the rain. I bring them up onto the porch and park them on the blanket where Velcro sleeps and where he sometimes rests while outside. Occasionally Master will go outside in the afternoon and find a whole pile of them in Velcro's bed. I guess he thinks the poor kitty will get upset because he moves them, but Velcro told me it's okay with him, the sticks won't bother him so long as I use them to scare snakes with. He got bit once himself. Anyway, I put them there so Master won't burn them up in the Franklin stove by using them to start fires with.

I should mention here that Cutie Pie died when I was about a year old, and Velcro inherited her bed. Master has long since discarded the cardboard boxes. There is now a regular wooden box with one end open for Velcro to sleep in. Or me, when the people are gone and the thunder monsters strart roaming around. I figure they can't get me if I'm in the box, especially if I pull Velcro in on top of me.

Sometimes I bring huge branches (huge to me, anyway) up onto the porch. Master has watched me struggle for an hour trying to haul a three foot long, two pronged branch up onto the porch and not given me a bit of help. I don't know why, since I have a definite purpose for them. I think they would work to scare a big snake off if one come on the porch, or keep a thunder monster from crawling in the cat box with me when I'm hiding there, but I guess Master doesn't agree because I no sooner get them onto the porch than throws them back into the yard. When I'm bringing them onto the porch, one of the prongs will invariably get hung up since I can't maneuver the big sticks too well and I don't like the idea of backing up and dragging the stick with me. I'd rather do it the hard way, as a test of my abilities. You never know when a dog might need a big two-pronged stick for all kinds of things; snakes and thunder monsters or maybe I might use it to tangle up a big bobcat's feet if one came on Cutie Pie's porch. I always try to do it sideways. Master thinks it's because of what he thinks is a little one track, two celled brain, but my brain is really full of determination. I won't stop until somehow I manage to get my big stick or branch onto the porch and safely secured on Velcro's bed. Then I will promptly go out and hunt down another one, just to be on the safe side.

146

BARKING

For a while Master and Mistress thought again there must be something seriously wrong with my jaw, and not just from the way I seem to have trouble eating and drinking. The reason they thought so is that they never heard me bark, even after I matured and my testosterone level was up to normal despite the one undescended testicle. Susie barked almost continuously, but all I did was growl, mostly in my sleep when the nightmares came. I made sounds, of course, so they knew I had vocal cords, even if I didn't use them to help them rescue me when caught in the chair or lost in the woods, but I've explained the reasons for that already. The real reason I waited so long to begin barking was because of the way they talked about that stupid Susie who barks day and night at nothing at all. I made up my mind I'd just wait and get them real worried about me before I ever uttered a bark, so they'd know I use a bark when it's needed and not for just anything or nothing the way she does.

Before I began to bark occasionally, it sometimes sounded to my people almost as if I were speaking some weird doggie language. That happened after I finally decided that rawhide chewies weren't going to poison me. Master and Mistress use the small size, naturally, since we are miniature dachshunds. I was very suspicious of them at first, and even after they finally found a kind I would accept (sometimes), I still had problems. They thought I didn't know how to lie down and hold a rawhide in my paws to keep it in place while I chewed. I pushed it all over the room with my mouth, trying to get it to hold still so I could chew on it. I could use my paws to make it hold still if I wanted to, but I think it's a lot more fun chasing it around the room and biting it than holding it down like Susie does. The small Dingo brand of rawhide chewies are the ones I like best. When I get tired of chasing them, they are small enough that they will at least fit between my front paws while I chew, although they frequently escape—and Susie the glutton is ever ready to steal mine once it gets out of range. She is quick as a striking snake with this trick, snatching my Dingo away before I know what's happening, especially since I can't see well to

147

begin with. Sometimes Susie won't even finish hers before she steals mine, which goes to show how mean she is. After stealing my Dingo, she will lay on her Dingo and chew on mine, appearing as if she is openly, deliberately taunting me—which she is, since she's bigger than me. Besides, I hate picking on females. They have enough problems without me being mean like she is.

Since Susie was bigger than me, that made her the alpha dog. Even so, I didn't take the thefts lying down. Or rather, I did take them lying down, but I had something to say about it. When she steals from me, I will lay on my tummy with my paws stretched out before me, as near to Susie as I dare, and begin complaining to our people about the unfairness of the situation just as plainly as a child wrongly accused of snitching a cookie. When that happens, I growl, whine, whimper, snarl, wherf, and make other noises, sort of like little woofs and snuffles and whiffles. All these sounds are mixed together so it resembles a dog language of some kind, with me lecturing Susie on how mean she is while she lies there silently, sometimes not even gnawing on either treat, just looking at me as if to say, *Yah, yah, I have both chewies but I'm the alpha dog; I can have both of them if I want to and you can't do a thing about it because you're not big enough.* That's how come I complained so much, because she taunted me about stealing and I have to complain a bunch before Master or Mistress will intervene.

I guess I was about two years old before I finally decided it was time to bark now and then, just to show my people I could if I wanted to and to keep them from worrying about it. They finally heard me utter my first bark. I looked up at them just as proudly as a toddler who has just learned to say da-da or ma-ma, even though it was really no big deal. I just wanted them to think it was. After that, barking gradually came easier to me until today I can practically burst their eardrums with my deep throated roar, a bark that sounds as if it's coming from a hundred pound German Shepherd instead of a little reddish black miniature dachshund. I guess I showed them who's the real barker in the family if barks are necessary, but Susie just overdoes it. My only problem is that most of the time I can't see what I'm barking at, so I when I feel like barking I just run in circles and bark at everything.

In the mornings when we go out together, Susie immediately makes tracks toward the far end of our three acre yard, barking at every insect, bird and varmint in sight, and if there's nothing to see she barks anyway, just on general principles. Once I decided to bark I do fine with the noise, but as I mentioned many times I can't see good so I can't tell what I should be barking at. I just run out onto the porch and turn in circles barking to the four corners with no idea in the world what's out there. Actually, I'm just announcing my presence to whatever might be outside, but Master and Mistress think it is really funny looking while they think I'm trying to act fierce. Master and Mistress kid each other, saying "Look at him. He thinks he's a real dog!" By golly, they ought to have to yell sometimes without being able to see what they're yelling at and it wouldn't be so dern funny to them. Of course I'm a real dog; I just march to my own drummer, so there!

I sometimes imitate Susie and bark to announce the UPS truck. With Master being a writer, it arrives so frequently that Susie's UPS bark is distinctive, just like her snake bark, so I thought I ought to get in on the act. With me they usually can't tell much difference regardless of what I'm barking at or whether I'm barking at anything. They all sound pretty much the same to them. But at least I do bark now, just to keep them from worrying. For a while they thought I would never learn, but I knew how to begin with. I just didn't want to act like that stupid Susie who barks all the time.

MY COLOR

Dachshunds come in different colors as well as different sizes. Some are long haired and some have short hair. The one familiar to most people is the short haired "red" dachshund, a color that's not really red but sort of auburn - a cross between brown and red. My people thought I was a red short haired dachshund, but as I grew the color and texture of my hair changed. A sprinkle of black hair began to grow in, mixed with the "red" along my back and down my spine. By the time I was two years old, the black sprinkles predominated, making my back and spine appear more black than red. The black fades gradually into red along my sides. Also I noticed that my hair was thicker and wirier than a normal short haired dachshund's usually is. When we get a bath Master and Mistress have to use an extra towel to dry me because my pelt is so heavy. As near as they can figure from dachshund books and breeders, I can be described as a cross between the colors referred to as wild boar and red. Truly, they couldn't find a picture of a dachshund that looked exactly like me, which they should have suspected since I'm so special. I'm an odd doggie in many other ways, so why not have an odd color and texture to my hair? Works for me! And to top it off, I go even further than that. When I collect a new scar—and I have plenty of them—my hair doesn't grow back in the same color it was before. Besides that, each new hair growth is not only a different color from the original, it is not even the same color as the hair that came back in over my other scars!

SLEEPING

Biscuit always slept in the bed with Master and Mistress, although it caused a lot of problems. He was such an active dog, and loved to dig for gophers so much that frequently he'd get into bed with them when they didn't realize he'd been out by the garden or in the Christmas trees, digging away for gophers. I've heard he even caught one occasionally, causing his eyes to light up like a Christmas tree ornament. Mistress put a pad under the sheets and they had to be washed frequently, but she and Master were a little younger then.

When Susie came along, they allowed her into their bed as well. She wasn't much trouble and she loved to snuggle up next to them with her head on whatever part of their bodies she could reach. Then they got me and now they not only had two dogs in the bed with them, but I couldn't get up and down by myself like Susie. I swear that little short legged girl dog can jump six feet in the air, flat footed. Well, maybe not quite that high, but she does amazingly well for a dog with such short legs, even shorter than the usual miniature dachshunds. Of course I can barely jump at all, or won't, which is the same thing since I can't see good, and that presented problems.

They started out with a regular bed which Susie could jump up on, then shortly after they got her they bought a larger pillowtop mattress, trying for something a little easier on their backs. Susie could still make it, but just barely. They were fearful of her *not* making it one time and falling and injuring her back, the kind of injury that led to Biscuit's death when he was only five years old. He died from complications of the surgery that they gladly paid $2,500.00 for in hopes of a cure, even though they really couldn't afford it. They'd do the same for me, of course, but I don't know about Susie. She's so worthless I would hesitate about spending much on her.

Mistress found an unused little wicker table that she placed at the end of the bed. That gave Susie a leg up and she had no problems after that. Me, on the other hand, couldn't jump that high even if I had been a normal puppy. I simply wasn't big enough yet. They fixed some little stairs for me but I refused to use them. I always saw two sets of them and was scared I'd try climbing the one that wasn't really there. They had to manually put me in bed and put me down the next morning, or when I scratched during the night to tell them I needed to go outside (scratching is another story that I'll get into shortly). Unfortunately, that didn't cover everything.

Dachshunds like to burrow. It's our nature, since we were bred first to be badger dogs. Naturally, we always want to sleep under the covers, which is fine with us. There is less chance of falling like that when shifting positions during the night.

I simply couldn't stay still under the covers because of twitching from nightmares, even if I didn't make noises. It wasn't because I thought the "cave" we all slept in was too large and I was looking for a smaller sub-cave somewhere under the covers. Whatever, it got me in trouble. I have said I seem to attract trouble, haven't I? My nocturnal wandering almost always led me toward the end of the bed since my people made sure I slept between the two of them. Otherwise, they figured I would slide out from under the covers on the side and fall and hurt myself, which was probably right.

Even so, I managed to get into trouble. Sometimes I would migrate down toward the end of the bed under the covers and fall down between the end of the bed and where the sheets were tucked in. Twice I wasn't in bed with them in the mornings. They looked everywhere, scared I had fallen out of bed and wandered around in the dark and gotten lost somewhere in the house again. Eventually they found me, fortunately the same day because I just stayed there, trapped but never making a sound because it was so embarrassing. It's hell not to be able to see good.

Another bit of trouble was me wanting to go out at night. I get attention by scratching but I discovered it was hard for them to hear me under the covers and wake up in time to let me out. On several occasions that resulted in me wetting the bed, something that definitely doesn't endear a doggie to his humans!

Besides that I was such an active little doggie, even as a pup, that I collected dirt in my thick pelt like "Pigpen," the Peanuts character, did on his person. Finally Mistress called a halt to the dogs sleeping with her and frankly, I was in agreement. Besides her worrying about me getting hurt, dogs living outside most of the day just naturally collect debris and I never liked bringing it into their bed.

The humans bought some beds for us but quickly found they weren't big enough for two, and me and Susie always seemed to want the same one. They bought bigger ones but it didn't improve the situation much. Finally they separated us from each other at night so we wouldn't argue. Susie sleeps in a corner of the bedroom between two of the big doggie beds stacked one on top of the other. It's a wonder the stupid female doesn't smother, but she likes it so who am I to say? I sleep in the living room in front of the fireplace. I like to be covered up with my blankie at night rather than burrow between two of the big beds like stupid old Susie does. Besides our sleeping beds, there's another big one out in the office we share peacefully when we're out there, and during the day we're usually compatible on my bed by the fireplace.

All this worked out fine—except that I got to where I expected Mistress to hold me for a while in her lap before putting me down and covering me up. A little petting before bed helps me sleep better and cuts down on the nightmares. Susie goes to bed by herself. She's lucky she never had a life like mine that causes bad dreams.

I guess all the bed shuffling proves that dogs are just as much individuals as humans are, as if we didn't already know it. Every dog that's ever lived in a house with people has taken on some human characteristics. We can't help it. Living inside with our people also provides more activity to occupy the minds of ordinary dogs like Susie. Me; I don't need it since I'm not the usual run of dog. I personally think that where it's possible, dogs are much better off living inside but people do take up a lot of our time, keeping them amused and happy. It's a dog's life, for sure.

SCRATCHING FOR ATTENTION

All dogs like human attention. We have evolved for it, after all, for over a hundred thousand years according to the latest findings. Most do it the traditional way by trying to jump up and put their front paws on people. If they've been taught they can't do that, they'll find other ways such as barking, running in circles, nudging and so forth. I heard that Biscuit liked to nudge Master and Mistress then sit up on his hiney and use his paws to gesture or touch them with until they figured out what he wanted. I think it's a shame dogs don't have vocal cords that can be used for talking. I'm managing it this one time to tell my story but it's real hard on my throat and I doubt I'll ever do it again. Most dogs know enough to go to a door and scratch or bark when they want to go in or out. Susie does that mostly, but not me. I didn't see good enough to learn to raise up and put my front paws on anything, much less a human, until I was over two years old, and was about that old before I decided to begin barking. I had to invent another method for getting attention. I taught my humans to notice me when I scratch and now I use that method for telling them just about anything I want or need. I like to scratch around on my bed before going to sleep, of course, but that's just normal, instinctive behavior for a dog, "digging a hole to sleep in" as we refer to it.

I scratch anytime I want attention or anything else, and leave it up to the people to figure out what I want. They ought to be that smart, I figure. Most often I'm telling them I want down from a chair. I'll also come into the bedroom at night and scratch on the rug on one or the other side of the bed (usually the mistress side) to indicate that I need to go back out to the bathroom. Occasionally they're sleeping so soundly they don't wake up in time and I pee on the rug, which serves them right—but I still scratch afterward to tell them how bad they were for not waking up in time. I'll scratch at the door when I want in but they seldom hear it because it's such a dainty scratch, done with one paw because I have problems using both at once while standing (unless I'm digging for something. I sure don't seem to have a problem then). Anyway, they need to listen closer is what I think.

A lot of the time I will come to the door wanting in and not scratch at all. I just sit on my hindquarters and look at the door, waiting patiently for it to open—and supremely confident that it will. I've got a way with it. If I stare at it long enough, it will open. The humans call it "waiting on the magic door to open" because my one track mind will keep me in that position practically forever, waiting on the magic door to open, or maybe my other brain cell is occupied with something else and I'm only using one to watch the door. If the magic door doesn't open after a long time I will occasionally have to make a noise, so I let them hear me make the most pitiful sounding wail in the world, as if I've been abandoned and think no-one will ever see me again. That gets them to moving, all right! It's very hard to describe that sound but it sure gets their attention. I am plainly telling anyone who will listen that I'm being mistreated and someone should do something about it. They have only heard me make that sound on one other occasion. That was when I got locked in the storeroom in the office from being so silently nosy. One of them went in there for something and didn't see me following. They heard me wailing from the living room as plain as anything. They think it's a shame I won't use that sound when I'm really in trouble, like when I got bitten by a copperhead snake again, but when I'm in trouble I like to keep it to myself and get out of it on my own if I possibly can.

SNAKE BIT AGAIN

This time it happened one Saturday night. Mistress had let me out for my next to last run outside. Usually I come back in before dark and don't go out again until just before hers and my bed time, normally about nine o'clock. Master has the early bird gene so he's usually in bed by six, having been up since three or four o'clock in the morning. At first I thought he was lazy, like Susie, until I found out he had that genetic defect. It made me feel closer to him since I have a few myself!

I didn't come in when it got dark, though, since a damned old copperhead snake had been crawling around at night when it should have been in bed like any decent snake--if there is such a thing, which I doubt. Anyway it bit me, because if I can't see well in the daytime I sure can't at night, and I never knew it was near me. Mistress waited and waited and I still didn't come because I couldn't walk and it hurt so much. She thought I might have gotten busy with something and my little two-celled, one track mind wouldn't turn it loose. She was sort of right because I was silently cussing whatever was responsible for snakes in the first place and wishing they would all go bite something bad instead of good doggies like me. Finally, after calling repeatedly, she took the high beam flashlight they keep by the door for just such occasions and went out to look for me.

I was easy to find. I was hardly a dozen steps from the door, laying half in and half out of a hole I had dug that day, looking for a mole or gopher--a rare occupant of our yard so long as we have cats--and never dreaming I would get bit by a snake and fall into it and not be able to get out. I couldn't move my back leg. Mistress picked me up and brought me inside then woke Master, who got dressed and they both examined me.

Neither of them could find anything obviously wrong other than I couldn't, or wouldn't, walk. Now that made both their hearts jump. Immediately, they remembered poor Biscuit and how they had thought a snake bit him when it was actually a disc in his back that had ruptured. And they also remembered how Biscuit had died after surgery, and how he suffered for a week at the Texas A&M small animal hospital, and how they suffered right along with him on that long 100 mile drive every morning to see him before coming back and opening the Christmas tree farm. With no obvious symptoms other than a little swelling of my back and hip, they just knew it was my back. I hate snakes. They are evil creatures that bite poor unsuspecting dogs who don't even bark at them like Susie.

Naturally, this was on a Saturday night. Doggies are just like human pups in this respect. They never seem to get sick or hurt during office hours or on a weekday. My people called Dr. Bob and got his referral service. Someone else was covering for him. They called there but didn't get an answer and sat waiting on a call back, getting more and more worried. They remembered Biscuit and how perhaps he would have lived had they known what was wrong with him sooner and got him into surgery quicker. Almost in a panic by now, they began searching for any place at all to take me, and all the time I was in Mistress' lap, looking first at her and then at Master, and silently pleading for help and wondering why they weren't doing anything. And I hadn't uttered a peep, not wanting to frighten them any more than they already were, even though I was really hurting bad by this time. It was just like when I was hung up under the chair. Silence. But now I wasn't embarrassed, or not much, but I didn't want to scare them.

Finally Master ran across a listing for a 24 hour Emergency Animal Clinic about 50 miles south of us, near Houston. They called to be sure they were open, then got in the car and headed that way. By this time it was almost midnight.

The clinic was open and I was seen quickly. Master and Mistress held their breath while the veterinarian examined me, still thinking it was my back and wondering what they would do if it was. They had already decided they wouldn't try surgery again on a back injury, not after Biscuit's experience. When the Vet said "Snakebite" it was a relief, almost the equivalent of saying nothing much was wrong at all. Shucks, snakebite? I could handle that.

And I could, after I got the usual injections and took them with my usual subdued aloofness. Soon we were headed home, with Mistress driving and me in Master's lap, zonked out from the shot for pain.

Now, by this time both of them had pretty well learned that I would eat cheese after a little coaxing, and I had decided that cheese probably wasn't going to poison me so long as it was placed on the floor first so I could sniff and peck and nose the first bite around for a minute or so to be certain it was safe. After that I would take a piece from Mistress' hand, then the next piece would come wrapped around a pill and the following one a normal bit of cheese, just in case I detected the pill the bite before. I did, but I always pretended like I didn't so I wouldn't hurt Mistress' feelings since she thought she was being so smart. The next day I took my pain pills and wobbled outside to relieve myself. By then they could finally see where I had been bitten, high on my hip. They figured I had probably walked right by the snake without seeing or smelling it and they were perfectly right. I had, but I still don't know why that snake bit me. Because it's a snake, I guess, and that's what snakes do. They bite innocent little doggies that can't see good.

GARDEN HOSES

I've mentioned that I likes to stay busy. When I'm not sleeping, I have to be doing something. My job with the pine straw slows down in the winter time when the pines have finished shedding and rain washes a lot of mud into the straw that's fallen, and the snakes are all holed up for the winter anyhow. Being work-oriented, I naturally devised another job for myself.

It began with Mistress watering the flowers in front, along with the hanging pots and the plants near the house. I'll get into the way I love to help with jobs later but for now let's stick with the watering.

First, I became convinced that the stream of water coming from the hose was just another part of the green limber "stick" she was carrying around. I decided to help Mistress carry it, since from my blurry viewpoint she appeared to be having difficulty with it. I continually tried to get a bite of the solid stream of water and nothing on God's green earth is ever going to convince me that it isn't possible. It looks solid to me so it should be solid, by golly. That's how the world is supposed to work, isn't it? So long as the hose is pouring out water, I'm going to try to get a grip on it and carry it somewhere. I refuse to go out in the rain to do my business but I will get absolutely soaked trying to get a bite of that water and not mind a bit, because I'm convinced it can be done if I just hold my mouth right and Mistress would quit moving that green stick around so much.

After the watering is finished, she thinks I'm convinced that somehow I succeeded in getting the water to stick in my mouth and put it somewhere, but that still leaves the rest of the hose, which is an oddly pliable stick to my little doggie brain. Actually, I know I never got a solid hold on the water and it just crawled back up inside that peculiar green stick. Mistress usually leaves it stretched out in the last place she waters, because it has to be done almost every day when it gets real hot and dry. That way she can start where she left off the previous day and not have to uncoil the hose. Ah, but that's not what I think! The hose is a stick and for some reason I never like the way Mistress leaves it. I'm convinced that if it's just positioned differently, that water will have to

159

crawl back out the end of it and I can get a good bite of it with it laying on the ground, so I immediately begin to try arranging it to my liking.

If there's no straw to work with, I may spend two hours tugging on different parts of that long hose, dragging it around until I'm finally satisfied that I've got it in its proper position and the water should start crawling out of it, but it never does, dern it. One day it will, though. I'm sure of it. It can't hide in there forever. I'm like an autistic in many ways, becoming fixated on a certain task and continuing with it to the exclusion of anything else until I'm exhausted, and that's one of those jobs I just hate to turn loose of.

But we can't leave the hose yet. I am an impatient little fellow sometimes. I don't like to wait—unless it's to check out something new in my food bowl before taking a bite, of course. I got tired of waiting on Mistress to finish watering so I could get the hose rearranged into its proper position to where the water would crawl back out. Mistress also has the habit of sometimes laying the hose down in order to clip a rose, or pick up something in the way or to tend to some other little chore. The first time she laid the hose down then reached to pick it up again she was surprised—it was no longer where she had momentarily put it. Impatient me was already moving it to where I thought it belonged. It got to the point where Mistress had to keep her hands on the hose at all times or she'd look around and I would be dragging it off, using all my strength to pull or tug on a section of it, bringing the rest of the hose with me, confident that if she would just leave me alone I could fix that water good.

It also got to the point that Mistress couldn't use the sprinkler to water her flower gardens, herb gardens and plants in the front yard because I am never satisfied with the way the sprinkler waters. As soon as she gets the sprinkler going and is satisfied it is working right, she will usually come inside and set a timer. After a while she began to get suspicious because it seemed as if the sprinkler was never in the same position where she thought she had left it, and naturally it wasn't because I had moved it. For a while she simply passed it off to short term memory malfunction, which happens to all people as they grow older, but it began occurring too often. She never saw me moving the hose, though, because I was sneaky about it. Then one day after she had the sprinkler going she came back inside and began performing a chore at the kitchen sink. Suddenly she jumped back in surprise. A torrent of water had hit the other side of the window looking out into the front yard! A minute later it happened again, and then she knew. The sprinkler had been moved. She went around to the front door and peeked through the panes of glass. Sure enough, there was I was, busily re-positioning the sprinkler. I was dragging it by the attached hose to a new area, where I was certain it belonged and where I still thought the water would come crawling out if I positioned it just right.

As I got older I began exploring just a little, usually over at Rob and Pat's house right nearby, before they got their own dog. One day Rob was washing their car and put his hose down for a moment to pick up a rag. For some reason, when he reached for it to begin washing again, it wasn't where he thought he had put it. He shrugged and went on washing his car but pretty soon the same thing happened again. He was beginning to think he was losing his mind because he hadn't seen me come over to help and still hadn't spotted me. Every time he looked away from the car, silent little me was out of sight and hiding from him. It was great fun fooling him. But the third time, he caught me. His hose had moved again, but this time he spotted an addled little dachshund rearranging his hose just like he did at his own house. My two-celled doggie mind didn't like the way Rob was positioning his hose any better than Mistress placed hers.

When Rob told my people about it, they all had a great laugh over the way I acted over at their house the same way I did at ours. A later encounter when Pat came over to visit with Betty wouldn't be such a happy one.

I ALMOST DIE

I've mentioned Rob's dog, Brownie. Actually, he turned out to be Pat's dog as much as, or more than, Rob's. After all, Pat controlled the treat bag, and Brownie's treats were much more restricted than those of mine and Susie. Brownie visited a lot by himself, especially in the morning. He made a regular circuit of the neighborhood, which I've described. He amused all of us by coming around in the morning when me and Susie and our people were inside the house. He was just big enough so that by straining he could get his front paws and head over the edge of the cast iron patio table where Master feeds Velcro, in order to keep me and Susie out of his food (not that I would stoop to eating cat food, but Susie might). Then he would quietly grab one of Velcro's food bowls and trot happily away with it grasped firmly in his jaws. He always took it back home with him and left it in his yard, where he had probably decided it might get filled if left there. When Master and Mistress finally caught him at it we all laughed at his antics and Master fixed it to where he couldn't steal the bowls any more.

Poor Brownie had come from a very "disadvantaged" environment, according to Rob. He had been badly abused as a pup. Once he began receiving kind and loving attention in his new home, he became very protective, especially of Pat. Unfortunately, none of us noticed it, simply because there was no occasion to.

One day when Pat came over to look at Mistress' flowers and chat for a while, Brownie came with her. I was outside with Mistress. I can't remember where Master was, but he had probably already gone to bed. As I've said, he has the early bird gene and lives about four hours in front of everyone else. Apparently I did something that struck Brownie wrong. I have no idea now what it was I did, but Brownie mistakenly thought I was threatening Pat and immediately attacked me. There was no warning and it wasn't just a scuffle, with Brownie trying to run me away from Pat. No, Brownie had death on his mind. He did his level best to kill me. He is easily three times my size, and although I fought my little miniature dachshund best, I was no match for Brownie. He quickly had me down and was tearing at my throat. Mistress and Pat

162

were both screaming at Brownie. Pat had him by the collar and was trying to pull him off me. Mistress was kicking and punching Brownie, and of course I was still fighting my little heart out, but it was all to no avail. The bigger dog was furious and was protecting his mistress, he thought. Pat took off her shoe and began beating him with it while still screaming, and Mistress continued screaming and hitting and trying to separate Brownie from me. Finally the combined strength of the two women got Brownie a couple of feet away, even though he was still struggling to get at me.

Mistress grabbed me up and ran into the house with me. Blood was streaming from my throat. Now remember, Master didn't see any of this. His early bird gene had already sent him to bed. He woke up and was out of bed just as Mistress brought me in.

It turned out that other than a lot of bites, cuts and scratches, my worst wound was a long gash on my throat, very near the jugular vein. A half inch closer and it would have been ripped open and I would surely have died.

Mistress was furious and so was Master. Since Pat and Rob live less than a hundred yards away we all knew that, inevitably, the same thing would happen again if something weren't done. And if it *did* happen again I knew that Master would shoot Brownie because if he didn't, Mistress surely would.

There was really only one solution to avoid the very real possibility of Brownie killing me and the equally very real certainty that Brownie would die very shortly afterward. And naturally, that would be the beginning of a family feud, the very last thing any of us wanted to happen.

Master and Mistress had been avoiding the subject of neutering me because I'm such a little fellow and had already gone through more trauma in my short life than most dogs will see in a lifetime. However, they decided the time had come and I reluctantly went along with it. Shucks, there weren't any lady dachshunds living nearby any more so it wasn't like I was using the things anyway. And not only would it keep me from one day losing my mind and following a female dog in heat away from the house and getting lost (the way Biscuit had done once), but it would perhaps neutralize my aggressive stance if I ever developed one. It seemed unlikely, but I had finally decided to bark and I would attack a single butterfly or a cricket if they threatened me or Master or Mistress, but I doubted I could ever be very aggressive because of my poor sight and one track mind.

Just neutering me alone wasn't enough, though. We were all still scared Brownie would repeat his actions, despite my changed status. Master took a walk over to see Rob when he knew he would be home, intending to offer to pay to have Brownie neutered along with me. Apparently he and Pat had been talking the situation over already because the decision to neuter Brownie had already been made.

Brownie went first, and I followed a couple of weeks later. Master and Mistress were very much afraid that relieving me of that excess baggage would turn me into a different kind of doggie of change my personality, or the trauma would set me back from all the progress I had shown lately toward becoming a "real" dog. Fortunately, it didn't. I retained the same odd and addled characteristics and my happy go lucky, one track mind, didn't change a bit. I still have the same personality and I still believe I am a real dog, albeit a most unusual one. I even try to act like one most of the time, despite all my handicaps. It just makes Master and Mistress love me all the more.

RUNNING IN CIRCLES

As I said, I did decide to bark sometime after my second birthday. No one marked the occasion so I don't know exactly when it happened, but one day Master and Mistress heard what they thought was a strange dog somewhere nearby. Remembering what Brownie had done to me, and scared that a new dog in the neighborhood might do the same, they ran out to look. And there was me. It was me who barked! I laughed a little doggie laugh at surprising them so much. Over the next few days I did it several times, until I had the technique mastered and my people got used to it. I would bark, then sit on my haunches and look at them with a happy expression and my tongue lolling as if to say *There! I did it! Aren't I a smart dog!* Of course it had taken me over a year longer to bark than a normal dog but nevertheless, they were proud of me. And besides, what's all the hurry about? I had proved (as if I hadn't already) that I could learn new things. I just had to get both those brain cells working at the same time, that's all.

Learning to bark and learning what I am supposed to bark *at* are two entirely different propositions, though, considering my stupid eyes. I never have quite got the idea. I usually take my cue from Susie, which as you know will lead to a lot of mistakes, at least close to the house. If Susie barks, so will I, usually, depending on whether I'm already preoccupied or not. Other times, I will be feeling exuberant and go to the door to be let out. Then I bound out onto the porch and run in circles, barking happily at anything and everything. Why not? I can't see a damn thing anyway. May as well bark.

The woods are about fifty or sixty yards from the front steps. Every day Susie patrols the tree line several times, barking all the while. She may even go into the woods and bark. Not me. I know the woods are filled with boogers and monsters and things that go bump in the night and I'm not about to get mixed up with them. I won't go into the woods! And if I can't see what's making a noise worth barking over, I won't run toward it like a stupid Susie does. I do most of my barking from the porch or from very near the house. The only exception was when a great big turtle tried to cross the yard and Susie spotted it. She got it cornered against the huge old pine tree out in the middle of the lawn and wouldn't leave the poor thing alone. She barked so continuously and furiously at it that finally I couldn't stand it any longer and went out to see what the fuss was about. I barked with her for a while but lost interest when the turtle remained in its shell. Not old stupid Susie. Master had to go out and pick her up and bring her to the house, then lock her inside until the turtle left before she drove us crazy with her yelping.

My people consider ourselves very fortunate that I haven't picked up Susie's bad habit of barking at everything in creation, 24 hours a day, but I'm not silly like her. I save most of my barking for things I can see, even if they do appear blurry. When I'm in the house and bark, it almost always means one of two things: Either Velcro is on the window ledge outside looking in and scratching or bumping the window or the UPS or Fedex truck has arrived, or possibly the mail. If they have a package too big to fit into the mailbox, the carrier will drive up to the house.

MORE RUNNING

As I grew older, I finally filled out to the normal proportions of a miniature dachshund. My people had worried that I would always be an undersized runt, and I'll confess, I had worried right along with them, but our fears proved groundless. I weigh in at a hefty sixteen pounds and nine ounces at maturity. Reaching my full growth proved to be a landmark in another area as well. Since my people think I don't know I am a real dog, I am always happy—except when the thunder monsters are booming and roaring out side. I am not only happy, but at times absolutely exuberant, and express my feelings by running in the house in order to show the humans just how I feel.

Our house stretches from the back door and office to the kitchen, and through a passage into the large combination living room and den, and terminates at the huge fireplace. I run from one end of the house to the other, back and forth, going full speed, and faster than it seems possible for my short legged little body. I run with my ears flopping wildly, my mouth open in a huge grin and my tongue lolling, the perfect picture of a stupendously happy and exuberant doggie showing off for his people. It's partly an act, just to amuse Master and Mistress, but most of the time I really am pretty happy with life, despite the handicaps I was born with. I think a smart doggie just has to make the best of what he has. Humans could learn something from me if they would.

At first I had problems with my poor vision and the hardwood floor. I have problems judging distances and I was constantly miscalculating and running into pieces of furniture, or skidding at one end of the house or the other and bumping full tilt into either the back door or the fireplace hearth. I soon figured it out though, because I run in a set pattern. I go straight from the back door all the way to the fireplace, then back by a different route that takes me under a chair, around a dinette chair and beneath the dining table, out from beneath another chair and around the passage into the kitchen, then into the office and under the computer desk and back out again and around the end of it and over to the bookshelves against the side wall, then around

167

the exercise machine and a sprint beneath a dinette table out there, around another chair and to the back door, where I start all over again. You fatty humans ought to exercise like I do and you wouldn't weigh so much!

I have learned to make this circuit at a dead run, slowing only as I near the fireplace and skidding into a complete turn that ends just short of hitting the hearth. How I manage all this with my poor vision is a puzzle to my people, but I do it. It's been a long time since I've run into anything or bumped my black snuffly nose that looks just like the front end of the space shuttle—and sometimes I swear I am going as fast as the shuttle does! I will run like this as many as a dozen times, stopping for nothing because I'm going too fast to see anything in time to avoid it. I just trust Master and Mistress and Susie to clear out of the way until I've run myself to complete exhaustion. I always finish up by my fireplace bed where I plop down to recover.

My people love to see me making my runs in the house. In fact, they even started encouraging me by saying *Run, Tonto! Run, Tonto! Run!* whenever I was doing it until now that's all it takes. They'll say *Run, Tonto!* and I'm off like I've been shot out of a cannon. They think it's always fun to watch and I never mind a little run when they want to see me go.

HELPING MISTRESS

When we dachshunds are in the house, which is about half of the time, Susie can almost always be found on the couch or a chair or sometimes in her cave of a bed, sound asleep. I may sleep part of the time, but if either of my people are doing anything besides reading or working at the computer, I am absolutely convinced that they cannot perform their tasks without my supervision. I swear, I don't know how they got along without me until I came to live with them, especially Mistress since she works harder than Master and besides, he doesn't like the way I type. He says I get the letters all mixed up, but they all look the same to me, so I don't know why he cares anyhow.

I am particular about helping Mistress sweep. I have to follow the movement of the broom and as soon as it has collected a little pile of debris, such as dog hair and the like, it must be inspected to be sure she's not sweeping up and throwing away something important. That entails walking in the pile, nosing it around, and in general scattering it back out so I can be sure it has been done right and nothing important has been swept up. I really feel put upon when I am relegated to the office with Master, behind a closed door, while Mistress re-collects the sweepings and finishes up the rest of the house. I don't care what she says, it isn't being done right unless I'm there to inspect it.

I also like to help mop to be sure Mistress gets the floors clean. The back and forth motions intrigue me, especially since it's being done with the aid of a great big stick with wet braches attached to the end of it. If there's anything I know everything about, it is sticks! It really aggravates me that Mistress won't let me get hold of that big stick with all the nice wet branches and let me show her how it is supposed to be done. Alas, back behind the closed door I go until the mopping is finished.

Folding clothes is another chore I wants to help Mistress perform. Shucks, almost any dog (except couch-potato Susie) likes those nice warm garments fresh from the dryer. Give a dog a chance at one of those and he'll run with it. Not me. I do it right. If Mistress inadvertently leaves an item of clothing on the bed within reach of me

169

(once I finally learned to raise up and put my front paws on something to keep me there) I will grab it all right, but I won't run with it. I will try to fold it up to show her how it should be done, even if it is terribly difficult to demonstrate with paws instead of hands! Naturally I will make a mess of it at first since doggies aren't really designed, nor equipped, for folding clothes but I will try, even if it means putting it on the floor and tugging it around and getting it dirty again, and if she would ever let me finish she would then know how it is supposed to be folded, but she always interrupts me. Happily, she doesn't banish me to the office because she is folding clothes. She just makes sure none of it is dangling from the bed she uses to sort and fold clothes on, drat it. I watch every step of the procedure with longing in my eyes, ever hopeful that one day Mistress may relent and allow me to completely finish showing her the proper way to fold clothes.

There's another place and another group of tasks where I am allowed he lend a hand... er, paw... that is. And that's the garden. Even Susie will bestir herself to go to the garden with Mistress and me.

THE GARDEN

When it's something one of my humans are doing, I'm able to shift gears rather quickly, where otherwise I stay on a single task until it's either done to my satisfaction or I have worked myself to exhaustion, and humans should take note of my fine work ethic and follow it themselves. I like to imitate (or do my little miniature best to imitate) almost anything the humans do in order to show them how it should really be done. They usually don't do things right if you ask me.

In our garden, greatly reduced from previous years, Mistress grows tomatoes, squash, red potatoes, broccoli and green beans. Earlier in the year she also plants lettuce and radishes. I'm not much interested in the early stuff like radishes and lettuce but I really loves to help till the garden and do the planting. I run up and down the fresh rows leaving paw prints everywhere, but after all I have to make sure the rows are done right and the only way to be sure is to inspect them and show Master where he got them crooked. I want to be present as each piece of potato is placed in the row to be sure the eye goes up, and I like to inspect the green bean seeds and the newly planted broccoli and tomato seedlings to make sure they've been properly planted. Sometimes I try planting one of them myself in order to demonstrate an instance where Mistress has gone wrong, but usually she does it pretty good and I'm content to just dig holes for them. Unfortunately, where I think the holes should be and where Mistress wants the holes dug are hardly ever in the same place, and it doesn't appear she will ever learn that she's doing it wrong and I'm the one doing it right.

I go with her every time she goes to the garden, afraid I will miss something new if I don't or that she will do something wrong and I won't be there to correct it. However, when I started licking the Sevrin Dust she sprinkles to repel insects and drinking the Miracle Grow she uses to fertilize with, back to the office I went. The Miracle Grow might not hurt me (at least I've drank some without ill effects) but they're certain the pesticide wouldn't do me any good. Oh well, neither of them are very tasty anyway.

I am allowed to help pick tomatoes and squash and green beans, and have lots of fun supervising Mistress with those tasks, but helping to dig potatoes is my favorite garden chore. When Mistress is out just gathering a basket of new potatoes to last for a meal or two I don't get to do much digging, but the complete harvest is altogether different. I am right in the middle of it, usually between Master and Mistress, digging and scratching and throwing dirt everywhere, and I actually am some help. I won't let them overlook a single potato that gets covered with dirt. I will find them every time and uncover them to show how careless they've been. If they're small enough I will even pick them up and put them in the basket—mostly. Sometimes I miss. Eyesight, you know.

I like to help with the yard work, too, unless it's mowing. In that case, I run pell- mell to the door and demand to be let inside the second the mower monster begins to roar. I'm not about to let that monster catch me and most likely have miniature dachshund for dinner. When Mistress is trimming bushes, I love to grab each trimmed-off branch and run with it—until I look back and see another one fall. Instantly, that distracts me and I abandon the one I'm carrying and run to get the new one. She really shouldn't cut so fast but she forgets how short my legs are and that I don't have time to get one branch positioned before she cuts another. There is an exception, though. It took only once to learn that rose bush branches are no fun for a little doggie to clamp his mouth on. Those thorns hurt!

LOST AT MIKE'S HOUSE

I said earlier that I didn't get lost again. Well, I didn't exactly get lost, but for all practical purposes I might as well have. What happened was that I only had one brain cell working that day. I had recently been severely chastised for trying to follow Truck and I would never do that again (well, I tried one more time much later but Master quickly let me know the rules still stood). That day, I saw their son Mike's truck pass our house on the way home, almost a half mile on back on our private road. I reasoned that neither Master nor Mistress had ever said anything about following a truck in that direction, especially a truck I recognized by the sound since Mike stopped frequently to visit. Besides, me and Susie had recently been accompanying Master and Mistress on their walks, which always stopped at the cattle guard where Mike's property line begins. They never went past there because they didn't want me to go wandering on down the road. Mike and Linda's property drops off in back to a Cypress Break, a gloomy, swampy place right out of something from a horror movie. Big alligators live back there, as well as wild hogs and wildcats and big boar coons and possibly a cougar wandering through on rare occasions, although Master hasn't seen it but once the whole time we've lived here. Anyway, they knew sure as shootin' that if I ever got lost down there I'd likely never be seen again. But I sure was curious about what lay on the other side of that cattle guard.

One day when Mike came home at noon, I got it into my head to follow him home—and I did. When Mike saw me, he immediately tried to run me back to our house, but I was already out of my territory. As I've said, I only had one brain cell functioning that day and besides, I figured as long as I was there I might as well see all I could. The best way I could think of to do that was to run around Mike's house. And I did, with Mike chasing me around and around it until we were both exhausted. It was lots of fun.

After the impromptu race finally stopped and we had each recovered, Mike finally got me headed back down the road toward our house. He told me forcefully, in no uncertain terms, to keep going. I went only until Mike was out of sight but then stopped. Even being on the road, I had forgotten the way home! Mike caught me sneaking back to his house and again got me running back down the road but, again, I only went until Mike stopped chasing me and then began going back toward the only house I knew the location of—Mike and Linda's place. I figured if I persisted, Mike would take me home.

Once I had seen all I wanted to, I finally allowed Mike to pick me up. He put me in his truck and took me back to his side of the cattle guard to where our garden was in sight. He thought that ought to be far enough so that I could find my way on home, but he had forgotten that I couldn't see well. And poor little addled dachshund me still hadn't gotten that second brain cell in gear. Besides forgetting the way home, I had forgotten how I went around the cattle guard the first time. Mike found me there a couple of hours later gazing longingly at the other side of the cattle guard but unable to figure out how to cross it.

Sighing, Mike picked me up and carried me halfway to the garden and put me down, and finally that did it. I spotted the garden and from there I knew the way. Gratefully, I scampered for home. I had been away for several hours. My people had just missed me and were getting ready to go looking, when I came running up to them, just as if nothing had ever been wrong! I didn't know how to tell them about my big adventure with Mike. They didn't know there had been an adventure until he told them about it a few days later.

I never ventured that way again. My people think it is the cattle guard that stymies me and that I don't have sense enough to go around it, even though the shallow gulley it crosses is dry almost all the time, and I'm certainly too small to go over it. I would fall through and probably stay where I landed until someone came along and found me. Actually, if I wanted to get my other brain cell to working I could find my way around the cattle guard but I've already seen all there is to see up that way now so I'm not interested in going back.

ESMERALDA

A befuddled dachshund hasn't got much use for anyone except his Master and Mistress. I'm not belligerent and never threaten anyone who's visiting. I just avoid them and won't allow himself to be petted, and certainly not held. Shucks, I didn't even feel easy about Master and Mistress holding me until I was well over two years old! I had gradually become accustomed to our regular visitors, mostly the kids and grandkids since we're pretty isolated out here. I will approach them and let them touch me for a minute or two, but that's about all. With the grandkids and great grandkids, I remain suspicious because they aren't that bright and might hurt me. I won't play with them or have much to do with them at all. When they're around I go into another room or outside and let Susie have all the attention. She loves it anyway so why not?

There's one exception. Sometime around my third birthday, Mistress decided to hire someone to help her with the floors and a few other household tasks that were becoming a bit wearing for her. Mrs. Luna, the lady they employ, usually brings along her ten year old daughter, Esmeralda. She is a quiet, sweet little girl and so gentle and polite and soft spoken you hardly know she's around. Everyone was astounded when I made friends with her almost immediately. I let her pet me, lay down with me and hold me and in general do just about anything she wanted because I could tell how smart she was and how well she knew how to hold and pet a dachshund. I still wasn't playful with her but I never tried to get away from her, either. Everyone was amazed.

They were even more amazed when Mrs. Luna returned on her regular Saturday morning house cleaning visit three weeks later and I remembered Mrs. Luna and Esmeralda. They figured I must have had both brain cells working the day I met them. And again, I let Esmeralda do just about anything she wanted to with me. In case you want to know, it's like you've read. Smart dogs like me have an innate sense of who they can trust not to hurt them, even inadvertently, as children often do with pets. At any rate Master and Mistress think it is touching to watch the two of us lay down and take a nap cuddled together, or to watch me follow Esmeralda from room to room as she plays or reads or sits on the floor and waits for me to join her. At last I have found a real human friend besides my people. They just wish they could afford to have them over more often or that they lived nearby so Esmeralda could come over to play with me after school.

PLAYING

I've told about me teaching Master to fetch. After that, my one track mind wanted him do it frequently, but Master and Mistress can only pay so much attention to me. They have their work to do (as I'm demonstrating by having Master write this while Mistress cooks supper) and Mistress has lots of chores to tend to around the house. That only leaves Susie, the couch potato who has never shown the slightest inclination toward play until recently.

I tried numerous times as I was growing up, and after I matured, to entice Susie into playing with me. She showed no interest at all, ignoring me for the most part—unless she saw a chance to swipe some of my bologna and cheese.

Master and Mistress are not even sure what started it, but after two and a half years Susie gradually began to play with me. They think maybe she figured out by that time I wasn't going to leave or get lost and stay lost, but what made her start to play was that she saw me getting more attention than her and decided to butt into the act. At any rate it began with her occasionally running back and forth through the house with me. That's all she would do, and all they thought she would ever do, until one day I picked up one of my toys and rubbed it in her face as I often did, trying my best to get her lazy old bones up to play with me. Master and Mistress' eyes widened with astonished surprise when they saw Susie grab the toy and both of us take off running, each with a hold on the stuffed monkey.

That was the start. Now we play a lot, grabbing stuffed animals and playing keep away from each other, or each grabbing a piece of a stuffed animal or squeaky toy and running with it together. Or just running together, with each trying to knock the other off our short little feet. Our people bought more toys and we have fun with them all now that I've finally got Susie to moving. We even have a toy box and Susie is the culprit who is constantly taking them out of the toy box and scattering them about the office, where we have a day bed and where the toy box is kept. I've got enough sense to know it just makes work for Mistress but Susie isn't that bright, as I've said numerous times.

177

Our people were very glad to see us playing together, of course. It made me seem more like a real dog instead of some mutant animal disguising itself as a miniature dachshund.

LAP TIME

I've referred to the thunder monsters and how my people have to hold me in their lap until they're gone. At first that was the only lap time I liked—or would even tolerate. But as I approached the end of my third year with my people, I got both brain cells working at the same time and made a couple of observations. First, I found out there was plenty of room for me and Mistress both in the new easy chair she got for her birthday, and in Master's chair, when I was hiding from the thunder boogers, I discovered something even better: a heating pad! Personally, I think he had just been hiding it from me all this time in order to keep from picking me up and setting me back down so often, but maybe not. Anyway, I'll give him the benefit of the doubt.

Master almost always has the heating pad going in his chair to help relieve the Sciatica that plagues him. It's nice and warm and I found that I liked the coziness of the warm pad as much as he does, besides the chair being a nice place to be protected from the thunder. In fact, it's gotten to the point that whenever I find Master out of the office and relaxing instead of working at the computer, I want to get up in the chair and stretch out beside him, with my little hinny firmly ensconced on the heating pad. The only problem is that Master refuses to let me up while he's either eating or reading the newspaper. I guess he's afraid I'll steal some food or read his paper first. It's hard for him to say no to me a lot of the time, though. After making him tell me umpty-leven times to "turn around" when he's ready to help me into the chair (so that I'm positioned in a way where there's little risk of hurting my vulnerable dachshund back) he finally learned that when I assume the position, I want in the chair. He'll be sitting there reading and happen to look down and there will be me, turned around and looking back over my shoulder, waiting patiently for him to notice me and pick me up, just like I wait patiently on that "magic door" to open. Not knowing how long I've been waiting in that stance makes him feel guilty and makes it hard not to go ahead and put me up on the chair. Susie can jump up on a chair whenever she feels like it but I don't think I will ever learn that trick, just like I doubt I'll ever hold a bone or rawhide down with my front paws while I chew on it like a normal dog does. That's because I'm not a normal dog, of course. I'm special.

From being held while the thunder monsters are roaming around outside to sitting on the heating pad, this little dachshund has graduated to having to be held by Mistress and rocked to sleep each night before she carries me to my bed in front of the fireplace and covers me with my blankie. I've really got them trained well. And in the morning after I've gone out to relieve myself and come back in, I insist on having Master cradle me in his arms and rub my tummy and under my arms and scratch my floppy ears for five or ten minutes. He's so well trained now he does it without me even asking him to, which proves humans can learn lots of things if you're patient with them.

I like tummy rubs, but being an odd doggie, I naturally have to be different. Other than that first rub while being cradled in the early morning, any tummy rub after that has to be done with a human's stockinged or bare feet, after removing their sandals, of course. They learned that trick all by themselves, without me hardly having to teach them at all. When I want a rub, which I do pretty often, I roll over on my back and wiggle around, waving all four feet in the air, waiting impatiently for Mistress to remove her flip flops or Master his sandals and give me a belly rub. I think I prefer Master to do it since he wears socks with his sandals while Mistress is usually bare footed except for flip flops. I won't settle for just a little rub, either. It has to be thorough, from beneath the chin all the way to my hind legs. I've taught them to always be careful to brace themselves with one hand on some nearby piece of furniture so they don't slip and accidentally put all their weight down on me. That wouldn't do a miniature dachshund any good at all!

MONSTER ON THE PORCH

One evening Mistress was attempting to put Susie and Tonto me outside for our last run of the night. Susie ran on out and went about her business, not forgetting to bark every few seconds, of course, but I stopped at the entrance. There was something there! I whimpered and would go no further. She attempted to nudge me on out the door with her foot but I wouldn't move. She told Master it was like trying to push a wet noodle, one that was whimpering and cringing and resisting the push. I flat refused to go further than the doorway. Finally she bent down to pick me up and then she saw what I saw, right outside on the porch. There it crouched, fangs bared and ready to eat me alive, a huge ferocious toad frog at least two inches long! I don't know why, because it wasn't the least bit funny, but she laughed herself silly before finally taking pity on me and moving that mean old toad frog. Then, with the danger taken care of, I went on out. But I wasn't about to face that ferocious beast head on!

CONCLUSION

As of this writing I am about five years old. Dachshunds and other small dogs usually live long lives. Dachshunds are vulnerable to back injuries because of their mile long string of vertebrae--well, it seems like we have that many sometimes. If a dachshund is going to have back problems, they usually occur around the fifth year (Biscuit died at five years old from complications of back surgery), but they can happen any time. I scare my people the way I run so vigorously and twist around in such sharp circles when I'm barking at boogers but I'm not going to try to contain myself. I'm such a happy little fellow despite my handicaps that it would break my heart not to be able to run and play and work. Perhaps my back will never bother me, and I've lived through so many life threatening events already that I have hopes of me just going on and on. In fact, if I live out the normal lifespan of a small dog, I may actually outlive my people!

I don't worry about it, though, and I'm pretty sure my people don't. I have more important things on my little two-celled mind than worrying about how long any of us are going to live; like going to work, helping Mistress in the house whenever I get a chance, playing with my girl friend Esmeralda and rolling over and getting that tummy rubbed with feet.

So happy days, as Master and Mistress tell me. May the rest of your life be long and enjoyable. I have already become known to people around the world through Master writing about me and using me as an example of the dachshund in his book *Bark!* and now I'm about to become even better known. Perhaps even famous! And it would be nothing more than I deserve, that's for sure.

THE END